SEBASTIAN ROOK

VAMPIRE
Plagues

EPIDEMIC

SCHOLASTIC

With special thanks to Helen Hart

To Ritchie Garrod, a great guy and a great nephew

*Thank you to Tom Dyakowski and
Mika Cichocka who helped with the Polish translations*

Scholastic Children's Books,
Euston House, 24 Eversholt Street,
London, NW1 IDB, UK
a division of Scholastic Ltd
London ~ New York ~ Toronto ~ Sydney ~ Auckland
Mexico City ~ New Delhi ~ Hong Kong

First published in the UK by Scholastic Ltd, 2005
Series created by Working Partners Ltd

Copyright © Working Partners Ltd, 2005

10 digit ISBN 0 439 95952 7
13 digit ISBN 978 0439 95952 0

Typeset by Falcon Oast Graphic Art Ltd
Printed and bound by Nørhaven Paperback A/S, Denmark

10 9 8 7 6 5 4 3

The right of Sebastian Rook to be identified as the author of this work
has been asserted by him in accordance with the
Copyright, Designs and Patents Act, 1988.

Papers used by Scholastic Children's Books are made from wood
grown in sustainable forests.

CHAPTER ONE

LONDON, LATE DECEMBER, 1850

On a crisp, cold winter's morning, Jack Harkett stood by the drawing-room window with his hands in his pockets, gazing out at Bedford Square. A lean and wiry boy with thick brown hair, Jack looked quite comfortable in his starched shirt, grey breeches and polished leather boots, despite having spent most of his twelve years barefoot and wearing little more than street-urchin rags.

Outside in the Square, ankle-deep snow lay like a thick white blanket over the cobbles, marked in places with footprints. Jack could just about make out the trampled patch of snow where a couple of days ago he'd had a snowball fight with his two best friends, Benedict and Emily Cole.

Reaching up, Jack eased the casement open an inch or two. Cold air rushed in and he sniffed it, wondering whether there would be any more snow before nightfall.

Emily Cole's teasing voice came from behind him. "Don't tell me – you can smell another snowstorm approaching!"

"Course I can," Jack declared with a grin. He turned to look at his friend.

Emily was sitting in an armchair near the fireplace, idly turning the pages of a book that Ben had given her for Christmas. Her feet were tucked up under several layers of white petticoats and a long, dark-red dress.

"Jack, for the hundredth time, you can't *smell* snow!" Emily insisted, laughing as she pushed back a lock of her auburn hair.

"Yes, you can!" Jack said good-humouredly. "You learns to read the weather when you have to sleep rough and live on your wits."

He sauntered across the room to stand in front of the fire, holding his hands out to the flickering warmth. A heavy gold ring gleamed on the middle finger of his right hand – a legacy from Molly, the motherly woman who had smuggled scraps of food to Jack during his years of hardship. Poor Molly had died a few weeks ago, and her grandmother's ring was all Jack had left to remember her by.

"Talking of snow," Jack muttered. "I hope my little mate Henry is keeping himself warm in this weather."

Emily glanced up from her book, her green eyes sparkling. "Henry enjoyed himself at our party yesterday, didn't he?" she said, smiling.

"I think if he'd eaten any more of that roast duck he'd have started quacking!" Jack replied with a chuckle.

Just then the drawing-room door swung open and Ben came hurrying in, a look of excitement lighting up his usually serious face. At thirteen, Ben was ten months younger than his sister, but already a few inches taller. He had neatly-parted fair hair and grey eyes. Like Jack, he was wearing a starched shirt, breeches and leather boots.

"Em! Jack!" he cried. "A letter's just arrived – I think it's from Uncle Edwin!"

Jack knew that "Uncle" Edwin wasn't the Coles' real uncle, but their godfather. He'd become their legal guardian when they'd been orphaned by the death of their father, Harrison Cole. Edwin Sherwood was an archaeologist and he had been Harrison Cole's closest friend as well as his colleague. Together the men had explored some of the world's most dangerous and uncharted regions.

"Uncle Edwin's travels have taken him to Poland," Ben exclaimed excitedly as he scanned the letter. "Listen to this. . . 'The conference in Kiev earlier this month went very well, and my research findings were greeted with intense interest by my esteemed colleagues. As a result, I have been invited to be a key speaker at the Royal Symposium of Archaeology and Anthropology in Poland in a few weeks. As you will see from this note-paper, I am staying at the Hotel Syrena in central

Warsaw. The city is wonderful! There is plenty to see, and the Polish people are very friendly and welcoming – the three of you would find it fascinating. I wish you were here.'"

Jack frowned. "What's a 'symposium'?" he asked.

"Same as a conference," Emily said. She had thrust her book aside and was sitting up straight in her armchair, her gaze fixed on the letter in Ben's hand. "Basically, famous explorers get together in a big lecture hall and give talks about ancient civilizations."

"And they'll discuss important new discoveries," Ben put in, coming to perch on the edge of the couch next to Jack. He was still looking at the letter in his hand. "Uncle Edwin says here that he wants to present a paper on Ancient American peoples."

"Oh, right." Jack nodded. "Like the Mayan folk in Mexico."

"I imagine Uncle Edwin will want to leave some things out of his talk on Ancient Mayans," Emily said thoughtfully. "Camazotz, for instance."

Camazotz. . . Just hearing the word spoken aloud sent a shiver down Jack's spine.

He, Ben and Emily had spent the last few months caught up in a desperate struggle against the Ancient Mayan demon-god, Camazotz. Their adventures had taken them to Paris, and eventually Mexico, where they had finally defeated Camazotz and his evil vampire servants.

4

Recently, however, there had been other vampires to fight. A strange new evil had arisen in London just before Christmas: a different type of vampire called a "lampir". The three friends had battled against the lampirs with the help of little Henry, a street-urchin Jack knew from his years of living at the docks, and a new companion called Filip Cinska. Filip had travelled all the way from Eastern Europe on the trail of lampirs, the walking dead who stalked the streets after dark and sucked the blood from their unfortunate victims.

The three friends, along with Henry and Filip, had defeated the lampirs by luring them on to a sinking ship which they then set alight, destroying every one of the blood-sucking creatures, so that England was now safe.

"I imagine Uncle Edwin's trying to forget Camazotz," Ben muttered, glancing up from Edwin's letter.

"Yup," Jack agreed. "I know I am!"

The drawing-room door was half-open and Mrs Mills, the housekeeper, bustled in. She was a short, middle-aged woman with streaks of grey in her brown hair. Jack always thought she looked stern, and she certainly ruled the housemaids with an iron hand, but in the months since he'd come to live in Bedford Square, Jack had learned that under her no-nonsense exterior Mrs Mills was very kind-hearted. She had looked after Ben and Emily since they were babies, and now treated Jack as one of the family too.

"Camazotz?" Mrs Mills enquired, smiling cheerfully

from behind a big silver tray loaded with glasses of lemonade and plates of sticky chocolate cake. "Is that another friend of yours, like that lovely Mr Cinska who was here yesterday? I suppose with a name like Camazotz, he's from Poland too!"

"Er, not exactly," Jack said, exchanging an amused look with Ben and Emily.

"He's someone we met in Mexico," Ben said casually. Then he deftly changed the subject, "Mrs Mills, we've had a letter from Uncle Edwin – he's been invited to speak at a symposium!"

"Has he now?" Mrs Mills looked pleased as she slid the silver tray on to a side table. "How kind of him to write. Does he give any idea of when he'll be coming home?"

Ben shook his head. "He doesn't say, but I don't suppose it will be soon because the symposium isn't for another couple of weeks. Uncle Edwin's enjoying sightseeing in Warsaw at the moment. . ." Ben read aloud from the letter again, " 'There are medieval watchtowers, and huge lakes, and peacocks which strut about in the hotel gardens shrieking and keeping everyone awake at night.' "

As Ben read out the rest of the letter, Mrs Mills busied herself passing round huge slices of chocolate cake.

"Thanks, Mrs M," Jack said, taking a plate from her. As Ben reached out for his plate, Jack noticed that one of his friend's fingernails was bruised. Jack assumed Ben had shut his finger in a drawer or door.

"I'll leave you to enjoy your cake," Mrs Mills said, making her way to the drawing-room door.

"Thank you," Ben said absently, as Mrs Mills left the room. He was still intent on the letter. "Listen to this, 'Speakers from all over the world have been invited to contribute, including Sir Peter Walker, the eminent historian'. . ."

"Sir Peter!" Emily's eyes twinkled with amusement. "I wonder if he's recovered from his brush with a 'lampir' yet?"

It had been Sir Peter Walker who had first freed many of the lampirs trapped in their graves. The historian had recently returned from a trip to Poland, bringing with him many antiques and ancient artefacts. Among them was an old bronze church bell that he'd found in a Warsaw monastery. The "Dhampir Bell", as it was known, was the source of many legends. It was said that if the bell was rung then the dead would wake . . . and lampirs would walk the earth.

However, Sir Peter had not believed in lampirs. He scoffed at what he called "superstitious nonsense" and rang the bell at a crowded lecture hall in Mayfair. The dead had indeed risen from their graves, and the lampir plague had quickly spread across London. Terrified, Sir Peter had retreated to his country mansion, taking the Dhampir Bell with him. The friends had been forced to use ingenious methods to retrieve the antique bell, which was vital to their plan for defeating the lampir plague.

Jack licked chocolate cake off his fingers as he remembered the night he and Filip had faked a lampir attack to convince Sir Peter to give up the bell. "Sir Peter was terrified," he said with a chuckle. "He'd have a fit if he knew that that 'lampir' was just Filip in white theatre make-up!"

"Well, the trick worked," Emily said with a smile. "And now Filip is going to take the Dhampir Bell safely back to Poland, where it belongs."

Ben folded up Uncle Edwin's letter and slid it back into the envelope. "I think I'll write back straight away," he said. "I don't know how long it will take for a letter to reach Warsaw, and I want to wish Uncle Edwin luck before the symposium starts."

As Ben made his way across the drawing room to the small writing table set under the window, Jack glanced at Emily. "I don't suppose you'd listen to me read?" he asked.

Emily had been teaching Jack to read for several months now, and in return he'd taught her how to pick pockets – just for fun. She smiled warmly. "I'd like that," she said, and the two of them settled down side by side on the couch with Mr Dickens's *David Copperfield*. Jack began to read carefully, running his finger slowly across the page and stumbling once or twice over the more difficult words.

Outside, the sky turned a steely grey and white flakes began to flurry against the window pane. Jack nudged Emily. "Told you I could smell snow," he said with a smile.

Ben looked up from his letter and exchanged a grin with Emily. "Jack, for the thousandth time, *you can't smell snow*!" they chorused, laughing.

Then Emily frowned. "Ben, you've got ink all over your fingers," she said.

Ben glanced at his hands and tutted. "I'd better go and wash it off," he said with a sigh. "Mrs Mills will be after me if I get fingerprints on the furniture!"

Ben was gone for a long time, and Jack was just beginning to wonder where his friend had gone when the drawing-room door burst open. A white-faced Ben came hurtling into the room. He looked dishevelled. His usually neat hair was sticking up in spikes and his cuffs dripped with water.

Ben slammed the door behind him and leaned against it looking serious. "I've scrubbed and scrubbed," he said darkly, "but I can't wash it off!"

Jack felt a flicker of alarm. "Wash what off?" he asked.

Beside him, Emily put aside *David Copperfield* and stared at her brother, wide-eyed with surprise. "Ben, what on earth's the matter?" she asked. "You look as if you've seen a ghost or something."

"Or *something*," Ben said with an edge of panic in his

voice. "Look!" He held out his hands, palms downwards and fingers outstretched. Every nail was tinged with a dusky shade of blue, as if each one was bruised. At first glance the discolouration did indeed look like ink, but Jack knew immediately that it wasn't. This was something much, much worse.

"Blue nails are the first symptom of lampir plague," Jack whispered hoarsely.

Ben nodded. "I've been infected!" he said grimly.

CHAPTER TWO

Ben saw the panic on Jack and Emily's faces.

"It can't be lampir plague!" Emily cried, standing up and hurrying towards him. "They must be *ordinary* bruises!" She grabbed his hands and began to inspect his fingernails.

Ben shook his head. "Think about it, Em. . . I might have bruised *one* fingernail, but not all of them – not without noticing."

"If it *is* lampir plague," Jack said hesitantly, coming to join them. "And I'm not saying it is, mind. But *if* it is – how on earth did you catch it? Filip Cinska told us a person has to have very close contact with a plague-carrier to actually catch the disease."

Ben shrugged. "Maybe when we were all fighting lampirs on Christmas Eve?" he suggested.

"But don't forget that if a lampir is destroyed, then anyone who has been infected by it is cured. And we destroyed all those lampirs!" Emily reminded him.

There was a silence as all three of them mulled over the possibilities.

"Ben did have pretty close contact with a different lampir, though," Jack said eventually. "Remember the severed hand?"

The week before Christmas there had been a desperate fight in the hallway of the Coles' house, during which Ben had grabbed a knife and sliced off a lampir's hand. Although the lampir was destroyed, the severed hand had unexpectedly taken on a life of its own, and it had hidden in a present that Emily unwrapped on Christmas morning. . .

"I grabbed the hand, and wrestled with it before it got away," Ben said. "The nails were so long and sharp. Perhaps. . ." He broke off, shaking his head unhappily.

"Perhaps it scratched you," Jack finished for him. He reached out and peeled back Ben's cuffs, peering closely at his friend's hands.

"Anything?" asked Emily.

"Yup," Jack said grimly. "Look!"

They all looked, and sure enough there was a long, thin scratch. It was half-hidden in the crease on the inside of Ben's left wrist.

"How could I not have noticed?" Ben said with a groan.

"Nobody would have noticed a scratch that small," Emily pointed out.

"It may only be a small scratch, but it did the trick,"

Ben sighed. "Look at my fingernails! There's no doubt – I *am* infected."

"It must be different because you were scratched by the hand *after* we destroyed the lampir it came from," Jack muttered.

"And we haven't destroyed the hand itself," Emily added thoughtfully. "That must be why you're still infected."

"Well, let's find the hand and kill it," Jack said. "Then Ben will get better."

But finding the hand proved to be easier said than done. An hour later Ben, Jack and Emily had searched all the rooms in the house and checked every one of the iron rat-traps Mrs Mills had set, but there was no sign of the hand. Soon there was only one place left to look: the attic.

All three of them held candles in their hands as they gazed up the stairs towards the closed attic door. Their hearts were in their mouths.

"The severed hand is up there somewhere," Ben said. "It has to be." He glanced down at his fingernails. Did they look worse? Surely not. He hoped he was just imagining that the blue colour had deepened.

"Come on," Emily said. She squared her shoulders and started up the steps towards the attic door with her candle held high.

Ben and Jack glanced at each other, and then hurried after her. A moment later they found themselves in the attic, with the strong smell of mothballs tickling their noses. The room stretched the length and width of the house, silent and full of shadows. Trunks, crates and boxes were piled high either side of a wooden walkway covered with a long strip of threadbare carpet. There was just enough light to see the sloping roof with its bare rafters swathed in cobwebs.

They surveyed the scene. Rolls of old carpet leaned upright amongst the trunks and boxes, while faded paintings and speckled mirrors had been propped against the walls. There were plenty of dark places for the severed hand to lurk.

"Reckon it'll take a long time to check every nook and cranny," Jack said. "Shall we split up?"

Emily nodded. "You two take the left side of the walkway. I'll take the right."

Ben peered behind one of the faded paintings. But there was nothing there except cobwebs and he moved on, holding his candle high as he searched for the hand. In places he could see that there were trails in the dust, as if something had cleared a pathway.

Could those trails have been made by the severed hand? Ben wondered, feeling an icy chill run down his back. "It's cold up here," he said, beginning to shiver.

Jack looked up from a box of old Christmas decorations. "Funny," he said, looking puzzled. "I was just thinking how warm it is."

"Heat rises," Emily put in with a smile. "The top of a

house is always the warmest." She moved away across the attic, peering behind trunks and under a sagging old armchair covered in dust.

A little later, Ben shivered violently as another wave of icy coldness washed over him.

"You still feelin' chilly, mate?" Jack asked.

Emily glanced across at them both. "You look very pale, Ben," she said, sounding concerned. "I think you'd better sit down while we carry on searching."

Ben was grateful for his sister's suggestion, because his legs were beginning to feel heavy and weak. Wearily, he sank down on to the lid of a nearby trunk and watched as Jack and Emily hunted round the attic. He wondered what would happen if they couldn't find the hand. What had Filip Cinska said? *A person infected with lampir plague usually dies after twenty-one days.*

Ben counted the time in his head. He'd been infected on Christmas Day, so that gave him until January the fifteenth. Nineteen days. And then he would die – and come back as a lampir! And *that* meant, Ben realized, with a sickening jolt, that he would have to make sure Jack and Emily had his body burned – before he woke in the moonlight and returned to the house, seeking his sister's blood!

Ben's morbid thoughts were suddenly interrupted by a scrabbling, scratching sound that seemed to be coming from inside the trunk. He held his breath and listened.

But the trunk was silent now. All he could hear was

Emily talking softly to Jack on the other side of the attic. Ben stood up and quietly placed his candle on a nearby chair. Then he crouched down and carefully lifted the lid, just a few inches.

Peering in, he saw that the inside was dark and empty – well, almost empty. Down in one corner he caught a glimpse of something claw-like. It was greenish-white with long, sharp black fingernails. . .

The severed hand!

Heart pounding, he shouted, "Jack! Em! Over here!" he cried. "It's the—"

But before Ben could finish his sentence, the severed hand sprang upwards out of the trunk and lunged at his throat.

CHAPTER THREE

Jack turned round just in time to see the hand attack. He let out a yell and dived across the attic towards his friend.

But, strangely, just as the hand was about to connect with Ben's neck, it twisted away without touching him. To Jack's surprise, it flipped backwards in mid-air, hit the floorboards with a hollow thud, and scuttled away in Emily's direction. Before Jack knew what was happening, the severed hand was crawling up the front of her dress like a huge crab.

Emily screamed and swatted at the hand. She desperately tried to hit it with her candlestick, but the hand evaded her every movement. It swung in the folds of her long skirts and heaved its way upwards.

Jack darted across the attic and swiped at the hand, sending it flying away from Emily. It landed on the ground, reared up on its wrist, and twisted to face Jack himself. But Ben was there, clenching his fists together and clubbing the hand with a blow that seemed to stun it for a second.

And that second was all Jack and Emily needed. Together they thrust their candles at the hand and it went up in flames. The rotten flesh was as dry as old newspaper, so it shrivelled and burned fast. Soon it was nothing more than a small pile of gritty grey ash, smouldering on the threadbare carpet.

Jack stamped out the last few orange embers. Then he turned to Ben with a frown. "What just happened there?" he asked, puzzled. "The hand seemed to change its mind about attacking you."

"I don't know." Ben's voice was weak. "But I'm glad it's gone."

"Lampirs can sense when someone is infected with the plague," Emily said quietly. "They won't attack one of their own, remember?"

Ben shuddered.

Jack patted his friend on the back. "It's over," he said. "We've vanquished the hand. Now you can concentrate on getting better."

The sound of the dinner-gong echoed up from the house below. Emily reached out and brushed a clump of cobwebs off Jack's shoulder. "Look at us, all covered in dust. We'd better get cleaned up before Mrs Mills sees us, or there could be some awkward questions!"

It was a relief to know that they'd destroyed the hand, and during luncheon, Jack could feel some of his

Christmas cheer coming back. He told jokes, and Emily begged him to share some stories about the years he had spent as a pickpocket, slipping through the crowds in search of a purse to lift, just so that he could buy himself a square meal.

Jack grinned and obliged, but all the time he kept a close eye on Ben, who didn't laugh like he usually did at Jack's jokes. And Ben didn't eat much either. He stirred his vegetable soup listlessly and crumbled a bread roll into tiny pieces, but hardly a morsel passed his lips.

Eventually, Jack leaned across the table towards his friend. "You feelin' all right, mate?" he asked.

Ben was staring down at the dish of raspberry tart that Evans the maid had placed in front of him. "I'm not sure," he said with a shiver. "I'm cold, so cold. And my whole body feels heavy, as if my bones are turning to lead. . ."

Jack and Emily exchanged puzzled glances. Why was Ben still feeling ill?

"Maybe recovery doesn't happen immediately?" Emily suggested. "It might take a few hours before Ben starts to feel better."

"I reckon that's it," Jack agreed. "You'll feel better later, mate."

But there was still no change that afternoon. Jack and Emily went up to Ben's room and found him curled into a ball on his bed, with the covers pulled right up to his ears. His face was pale and waxy, and when he tried to speak, he broke into fits of coughing that wracked his whole body.

"This ain't right," Jack declared, with an anxious glance at Emily. "He should be getting better by now."

Emily knelt by the bed and examined Ben's fingernails, which were now a dark blackish-purple. "Why don't you come downstairs and have some tea, Ben?" she suggested, smiling encouragingly. "Maybe you're just hungry. Cook's made an apple cake – your favourite."

But tea and apple cake didn't change anything, and by breakfast time the next day Jack was convinced that destroying the hand hadn't made the slightest bit of difference to Ben's illness.

Mrs Mills was beginning to notice that things weren't quite right too. She bustled into the dining room with a sizzling platter of sausages, took one look at Ben, and said, "Master Benedict, you're terribly pale this morning. Are you feeling all right?"

"I'm fine," Ben replied, tucking his purple fingernails under the table, out of sight.

But Mrs Mills reached out and gently touched the back of her hand to his forehead. "Dear me! Your skin is as cold as ice. I shall send Evans out to fetch the doctor!"

Jack and Emily stared at each other in alarm.

"A doctor won't be necessary, Mrs Mills. There's nothing wrong with me," Ben said firmly.

"It's probably just a chill," Emily put in. "After all, we

stayed out in the snow for a long time on Christmas morning!"

Mrs Mills sighed and nodded. "Maybe calling for the doctor would be a little hasty," she agreed. "I'll get Tillet to draw some hot water for a bath instead, and we'll put some mustard powder in. It might make your eyes water, but it certainly does the trick when you've got a chill."

Mrs Mills bustled off to round up the housemaid and find a packet of mustard powder.

"I don't understand – why am I not getting better?" Ben asked, frowning.

"I don't know," Emily replied, slowly putting down her fork.

"I reckon we need a bit of help with this," Jack said firmly.

Emily nodded and pushed her chair back from the breakfast table. "Jack's right," she said to her brother. "We need an expert on lampir plague. It's time we paid a visit to Filip Cinska."

Leaving a quickly-scribbled note for Mrs Mills, the friends wrapped up warmly and hurried out into the snow to flag down a two-wheeled hansom cab. Filip Cinska was staying in a rented room above a watch and clock shop in Tiler's Alley, south of the River Thames. During the journey Ben sat in the corner of the hansom, muffled to the ears in a thick coat and scarf, silently thankful that he'd managed to escape Mrs Mills's mustard bath – for now.

It was mid-morning when they arrived in Tiler's Alley, and a weak winter sun was trying to shine in an overcast grey sky.

Jack paid the cab driver while Emily helped Ben down from the hansom.

"I feel like an old man," he grumbled.

The three friends made their way down the narrow cobbled alley to the watch and clock shop. Filip's landlady, Widow Kaminski, gave them a disapproving stare, but said nothing as they hurried up the wooden staircase which zigzagged through her lodging-house, making for Filip's room in the attic.

Emily rapped on the door. There was silence, and for a horrible moment Ben wondered if they were too late. What if Filip had already taken a ship back to Poland?

But then the attic door was flung open, and a man in a frock coat and striped trousers peered out at them. He was about forty years old, small and wiry with an angular face and long nose. Wild blond hair stuck up in tufts all over his head, adding to his already dishevelled appearance.

"My friends!" Filip Cinska exclaimed, in his strong Polish accent. "Come in! Come in!" He waved them in enthusiastically. "How wonderful to see you again. I am so glad you caught me before I leave. I haf a passage booked on a steam ship tomorrow, and as you see, I am in the middle of packing."

They did see. There was a battered old suitcase open on the floor, and the small attic room looked as if a whirlwind had hit it: books and newspapers littered every surface, shirts and trousers were strung over chairs, and a pair of scarlet braces dangled from a hook sticking out of the sloping ceiling.

"Come! Sit down and be comfortable," Filip said. He began to haul some rickety stools out from under an equally rickety table. "Tell me: to what do I owe this very great pleasure?"

But before anyone could begin to explain, Filip made a startled sound deep in his throat and darted over to Ben. He took him by the shoulders and twisted him towards the window, where the light was strongest.

Ben flinched against the daylight, then waited as Filip studied him intently. He saw puzzlement, growing concern, and finally comprehension dawning on the little Polish man's face.

"You haf the lampir plague, my friend," Filip whispered in horror. "The symptoms are unmistakeable." He seized one of Ben's hands, tugged off his gloves, and examined the blackish-purple fingernails. "How did this happen?"

"We think he was infected by the lampir's severed hand," Emily told Filip. "Remember we told you that it leaped out of a box on Christmas morning?"

"Yes, yes," Filip said, nodding vigorously. "The hand tried to attack you, Emily. And Ben fought it off with great bravery. But obviously to his own cost!" He pushed the fair hair back from Ben's brow and felt his forehead. "You haf a feeling of great cold, yes?"

Ben nodded, and Filip went on, "You feel as though a tide of ice is sweeping through your veins. And you are tired, so tired. Your bones are made of lead and you wish only to lie down. Oh, it gives me great pain to see you like this!"

Filip led Ben to the only armchair, a sagging thing which stood in front of the pot-bellied stove. "Sit here and warm yourself," he insisted.

He cranked open the stove and fed in more coal, then turned to fix Emily and Jack with a piercing gaze. "So, where is the severed hand now?"

"We destroyed it," Jack replied, and Emily quickly explained how they'd hunted down the hand and set fire to it in the attic.

"And you say this was yesterday morning?" Filip murmured, looking troubled. "Then it is very strange that young Benedict has not yet recovered. Usually when a lampir is destroyed, the plague sufferer's recovery is almost immediate."

"Not this time, it ain't," Jack said. "In fact, I reckon Ben's getting worse, not better."

"And that's why we're here," Emily said, unbuttoning her coat and sitting down at the rickety table.

24

"We were hoping you might know what we should do."

As they talked, Ben shivered and leaned closer to the stove. He wished they would all hurry up and decide how to help him, because he didn't feel as though he could stay upright for very much longer. He needed to lie down, but at the same time the idea terrified him, because he remembered Filip telling them before Christmas that once a plague sufferer lay down, they never got up again. But Ben realized he was going to have to sleep over the course of the next few days. It seemed that never getting up again was a risk he would just have to take. Eighteen days, Ben reminded himself firmly. The infection wouldn't actually claim his life for another eighteen days.

Filip Cinska began to pace up and down, thrusting his fingers through his wild hair as he gave the matter some thought. "Kill the lampir that infected you, and you will recover," he muttered, more to himself than to the friends. "Always, this is the rule. . ."

Abruptly he stopped pacing and turned to point a long, bony finger at Ben. "But it was not a lampir that infected you!" he said slowly. "It was the *severed hand*. The lampir was killed many days ago by our courageous Emily." Filip frowned and rubbed his chin thoughtfully. "And with the lampir already dead, it would seem that the usual rules do not apply."

Hearing this, Ben began to shiver more violently. A deathly chill seemed to settle on his heart. He could see

Jack and Emily gazing at him with dismayed expressions on their faces.

"But why should that be the case?" Emily exclaimed, looking anxious.

Filip sighed. "I haf no idea why, Emily. But there is no doubt that your brother is still infected. And I am sorry to say that I do not know of a way to save him!"

CHAPTER FOUR

Filip's words were met with horrified silence.

Emily stared at her brother in despair. He looked terrible – there were dark shadows under his eyes, and despite the warmth from the stove he was shivering. "There must be *something* we can do to save him," she said desperately.

Filip shook his head. "There is nothing, unless. . ." He suddenly became very thoughtful, and strode across the room to peer out of the window across the snowy rooftops of London.

Emily and Jack exchanged a glance, but neither of them said anything. They knew better than to interrupt Filip when he was mulling over an idea.

At last he turned back to them. "You remember I told you about my brother, Roman, who lives in Poland?" he asked.

"Yes," Emily said quickly. "He's a doctor."

Filip nodded. "My brother is a very clever man who

has devoted his life to seeking a cure for the lampir plague. Every day Roman is in his laboratory making potions and testing serums. I am thinking that perhaps one of these potions might offer Ben some chance of survival."

Emily felt a rush of hope. "Then we must go to Poland and see Roman – we shall travel with you tomorrow, Filip!"

Jack bit his lip thoughtfully. "We'll have to think of a pretty convincing explanation for Mrs Mills," he pointed out. "She's going to have fifty fits when she finds that Ben's been out at all. She won't be keen to let him go all the way to Poland."

Emily glanced across at Ben, who was hunched by the stove looking miserable and ill. "Ben," she said gently, "you going to have to look and act as if you're completely healthy again, so that Mrs Mills will let you travel. Do you think you can do that?"

"I can *act* healthy," Ben replied bravely. "But I don't know if I can look it."

"I think I can help you there, my friend," Filip said eagerly, hurrying into an adjoining room and emerging a minute later with his bony hands full of small lacquered pots. The lids were painted with a variety of tiny Eastern European motifs: flowers, curling vines and little bluebirds.

Emily recognized the pots immediately. "Your theatre make-up!" she exclaimed. "That's what you used at Sir Peter Walker's, when you pretended to be a lampir."

"And it worked very well, did it not?" Filip laughed. "With a pale face and dark circles under my eyes I looked just as Ben does now. But this time, we shall use the make-up for exactly the opposite effect."

"You're going to make Ben look healthy!" Jack declared.

Filip moved across the room to where Ben was curled in the armchair. "With your permission, my friend," he said, crouching beside him, "I shall use pink paste to give you a rosy colour, and perhaps a little white under the eyes to lighten those dark shadows."

Emily and Jack watched, fascinated, as Filip went to work.

First, he took some white paste, diluted it with a few drops of water, and mixed it with the tiniest dot of red, gradually increasing the quantities until he had created a skin-coloured paste. He tested it on Ben's cheek with the edge of a small, wedge-shaped piece of damp sponge. When Filip was satisfied that he had the colour just right, he spread the mixture gently over Ben's face using tiny circular movements.

Soon the dark circles under Ben's eyes had disappeared beneath Filip's make-up. His cheeks had a healthy glow, and he looked perfectly normal.

Jack let out a low whistle. "Now that's what I call amazing," he said.

Emily smiled at Ben. "Nobody would know you're ill at all!" she exclaimed.

Filip sat back on his heels to check his handiwork, then he fetched a little mirror so that Ben could see the transformation.

Ben peered at his reflection for a long time, turning his head this way and that. At last he gave a weak smile. "Filip, you're a genius," he whispered.

Filip shook his head. "No, my friend. I merely spent ten years travelling across Europe with a touring theatre troupe." He smiled gently at Ben. "And now I have done all I can. The rest is up to you. Your Mrs Mills is no fool. You will need to give quite a performance if you want to convince her that you have recovered!"

The friends parted from Filip at the end of Tiler's Alley. He was going directly to the shipping office to book passage for Ben, Jack and Emily on the steam ship he was taking the following day.

Meanwhile, Ben was heading home with Jack and Emily to give the performance of a lifetime. As the hansom cab rattled over London Bridge he felt a small, round shape digging against his ribs. He smiled – in his coat pocket was a glass jar of pale-pink paste and a piece of sponge. Filip had pressed them into Ben's hands before they left the little attic room. "Just in case you need to touch up your healthy complexion in the morning," he had said with a wink.

Back in Bedford Square, Mrs Mills met the three friends at the front door. She had their scribbled note in her hand, and watched crossly as they climbed down from the hansom cab. But she softened instantly when Ben bounded up the steps and gave her a huge grin.

"You're obviously back to your usual self, Master Benedict!" she observed as she ushered them all indoors.

"Oh, I'm feeling much better," Ben replied, forcing himself to sound hearty. "I think a ride in the fresh air has helped me shake off whatever I was suffering from!"

"We've been to say goodbye to Filip Cinska," Emily put in, peeling off her warm, woolly gloves. "He's leaving on a steam ship tomorrow. And guess where he's going, Mrs Mills – Warsaw!"

"My goodness, that's where Mr Edwin is," Mrs Mills declared as she took their overcoats. "I wonder if the two gentlemen will bump into each other."

"Actually. . ." Ben glanced at the others. "We were thinking of bumping into Uncle Edwin ourselves."

Mrs Mills looked surprised, and Ben carried on quickly, "He told us in his letter how much the three of us would enjoy ourselves in Warsaw. It's a wonderful city, full of lovely old buildings and museums."

"Yes, a visit would be so educational," Emily added, her eyes shining. "We could meet up with Uncle Edwin, listen to some of the lectures, take a sightseeing tour, and then all travel home together!"

Mrs Mills looked doubtful. "I can see that an

educational visit would further your studies," she conceded, "but unfortunately Mr Edwin isn't expecting you."

"Oh, that's easily remedied!" Ben picked up Uncle Edwin's letter from the hall table. "We know exactly where he's staying; he wrote to us on the hotel's headed notepaper. Look, *Hotel Syrena, Castle Square, Old Town, Warsaw*. If we send a telegraph this afternoon, Uncle Edwin will get it by the end of the week. Imagine how delighted he'll be to discover that we'll be there to support him when he gives his key speech at the symposium!"

But Mrs Mills was still not entirely convinced. "Sending a telegraph is one thing, Master Benedict," she said, frowning. "But I simply cannot allow three young people to go gallivanting off across Europe, all alone."

"But we wouldn't be all alone, Mrs M," Jack reminded her cheerfully. "We'd be with Mr Cinska."

That settled the matter. Having met Filip during the Boxing Day celebrations, Mrs Mills had been sufficiently taken with his old-fashioned Polish manners that she was soon persuaded to trust him as a companion and guardian to Ben, Emily and Jack. And once persuaded, she was formidable in her travel plans: telegraphs were despatched, bags were heaved down from the attic, and Tillet and Evans were pressed into service with the packing.

Ben kept to his room as much as possible. But to

32

avoid arousing Mrs Mills's suspicions, he touched up his pink make-up that evening and bravely went downstairs for supper.

Jack grinned at him across the dining-room table. "You should be on the stage, mate," he whispered to Ben.

The following morning, Ben was feeling even worse. It was all he could do to dress himself, sponge pink make-up on to his face, and maintain a performance for Mrs Mills over breakfast. His legs were like jelly by the time Evans announced that Filip Cinska and a four-wheeler had arrived to take them to the docks.

Out in Bedford Square, Jack and Emily quickly helped Ben into the carriage while Mrs Mills had her back to them. She was busy fussing over the three leather bags that Evans and Tillet were heaving down the front steps.

Filip Cinska helped the coachman stow the luggage beside his own, which consisted of a single battered old suitcase and a big blue hat-box. "The Dhampir Bell is safely stored in here, my friends!" Filip whispered, giving the hat-box a pat.

Ben managed a grin in response.

"All set!" Mrs Mills declared, smiling at the friends through the window of the carriage. Then she stepped back on to the snow-dusted pavement to wave as the coachman cried, *"Ha-way!"* and the four-wheeler clattered off over the cobbles.

The moment they were out of sight, Ben slumped back into the corner of the carriage, exhausted.

Emily turned to give his arm a comforting pat. "Well done, Ben," she said warmly. "You did it. We're on our way to Poland!"

Ben nodded. He just hoped that getting to Poland – and Doctor Roman Cinska – would be enough to save his life!

CHAPTER FIVE

DANZIG, JANUARY 1851

Muffled in a greatcoat, scarf and thick woollen hat, Jack leaned his elbows on the blistered handrail of the lower deck of the great steam ship, *Saxonia*. He gazed out at the mid-morning hustle and bustle of the busy dockside. A raw, salty sea breeze tugged at his clothes, biting through the thick layers of fabric to chill him to the bone. But he didn't mind one bit, because the gangplank had been lowered, the luggage was being unloaded by porters, and in just a few minutes Jack, Ben and Emily would be able to disembark.

They had reached the Prussian port of Danzig, at last!

The little party had left London just over a week ago, with their trunks and bags, and the blue hat-box containing the Dhampir Bell that Filip guarded day and night. Three days on the steam ship *Konigsberg* had taken them to Hamburg in Germany, where they had stayed overnight in a dockside inn before boarding the *Saxonia*, which had chugged along the Pomeranian coastline for the past four days. They had quietly celebrated the turn of the year at sea.

Poor Ben had stayed in the cabin, weak and feverish. His performance for Mrs Mills seemed to have exhausted his last reserves of energy, and now it was all he could do to lift his head from the pillow and take a sip of water. Jack, Emily and Filip had taken it in turns to look after him.

On the previous afternoon, when it had been Emily's turn to nurse her brother, Jack and Filip had spent an hour out on deck. The two friends watched the rugged coastline slip past beneath the granite sky as Filip talked quietly about their destination.

"The Kingdom of Poland no longer exists except in name," he told Jack. "A long time ago, my country was carved up as the spoils of war between the vast empires of Prussia, Russia and Austria. Danzig is in Western Prussia, while Warsaw is part of the Western Territories of Russia and has been ruled by Czar Nicholas I for twenty years."

Jack raised his eyebrows. "So we land in Prussia and then travel across country into Russia?"

Filip nodded. "We will cross the border about halfway through our journey."

Now, as the *Saxonia* docked in Danzig, Emily came up on deck to join Jack. The velvet collar of her green coat was turned up to her ears and her hat was pulled down low. All Jack could see was the tip of her nose and her sparkling eyes as she watched the ship's crew heave trunks, bags and boxes up from the hold and out on to the busy dockside. A thousand voices rose on the air, some calling out in German, others in Polish. Jack had spent enough time listening to the sailors in London dockside taverns to recognize a word or two.

A tall man in a white coat and grey fur hat stood at the bottom of the gangplank and roared, "*Alles aussteigen!*"

"Come on," Jack said, nudging Emily. "We'd better go and get the others. The Captain's just given the order to disembark!"

Once they had their feet on dry land, Filip took charge, engaging a porter to take their luggage on a hand-cart to the nearest coaching inn. The party of travellers followed him on foot, the icy winter wind cutting through their warm clothing.

Away from the docks, they found themselves on a broad cobbled street flanked by prettily-painted buildings and graceful churches with pointed spires.

"So this is Danzig," Jack muttered, more to himself than anyone else. He loved to travel, but he regretted that his best friend had to be at death's door for his wish to come true.

The coaching inn wasn't far away. Jack soon saw the three-storey brick building, with a red-tiled roof and a yard strewn with straw, standing at the corner of the street. As they approached, their porter gave a sharp warning cry; an enormous horse-drawn stagecoach lurched out of the inn-yard. The friends drew back just in time, but Jack had to make a grab for poor Ben, who was looking dazed.

"I hope that weren't the Warsaw coach," Jack muttered, as the huge stagecoach thundered away down the street. "We don't want to be stuck here for days waiting for the next one."

But there was another coach in the yard, its dull black paintwork and huge iron-rimmed wheels spattered with dried mud. Four sturdy-looking horses with blankets over them were harnessed to the front, breath from their nostrils making clouds in the freezing air. Nearby, a group of expectant-looking passengers fiddled with bags and bundles while the inn-keeper bustled about.

He carried a tray of pewter mugs. "*Bier!*" he called cheerfully, which Jack knew meant, "Beer!"

Filip hurried over to speak to the coach driver, a burly, moustachioed man wearing a sheepskin coat, a fur hat, and a pair of baggy trousers tucked into his boots. A rapid-fire conversation in Polish followed. Eventually, Filip handed the driver a fistful of money and gave Ben, Jack and Emily the thumbs-up sign.

"This is the Warsaw coach," he called. "Our driver is called Kornel and he knows this route like the back of his hand. As does his groom, Bartosz." Filip pointed out a second man, kneeling up on the roof of the stagecoach, making it rock slightly as he tightened thick leather straps around a huge pile of baggage covered in green canvas.

Bartosz saw the friends gazing up at him and gave them a cheery wink.

"These men will make sure we get to Warsaw," Filip continued. "The stagecoach is leaving in just a few minutes. A stroke of luck, eh? We could not have hoped to reach the city so quickly! In four days' time we shall be sipping Polish tea with my brother, Roman." He peered at Ben, his face full of concern. "How are you holding up, my friend?"

"I'm managing," Ben muttered bravely. But he looked pale and his teeth were chattering.

"Come on," Jack said, taking his friend's arm. "Let's find you a seat inside the coach."

The boys climbed the iron steps into the stagecoach with Emily close behind. The dimly-lit interior was large and roomy. The ceiling and walls were lined with threadbare, musty-smelling velvet. There were two rows of padded bench seats and a hinged seat fixed to the far wall which could be folded down to take an extra passenger. The whole arrangement reminded Jack of a train compartment.

Underneath the seats were a series of square metal boxes with small holes cut in them. Each box gave off a pleasant warmth.

"Those boxes are full of hot coals!" Jack exclaimed.

"Braziers!" Emily grinned. "At least we'll be warm on the journey."

They found a snug corner and installed Ben nearest to the window with a brazier at his feet, though he still shivered with cold.

The other passengers began to take their places. There were about nine of them altogether, mostly peasant women in brightly-coloured headscarves, but also a couple of rich-looking merchants with fur hats and gleaming gold watch chains. They bustled about, swapping seats and making the coach sway as they stowed cloth bundles beside them on the benches, or tossed bags up into a net canopy over their heads.

Filip Cinska sat opposite Ben with the blue hat-box containing the Dhampir Bell propped on his knees. "So, my friends," he said. "The next leg of our journey begins. . ."

And with that, Bartosz the groom slammed the door and jumped up on to the footplate at the back of the coach, and the conveyance lurched forwards. It maintained a stately pace through the cobbled city streets. But soon they clattered under a huge brick archway touched with gold paint, which Jack guessed was Danzig's city gate, and then the driver whipped up the horses and the stagecoach thundered along the road at breakneck speed, pitching and creaking like a ship in a storm.

Peering past Ben to see out of the window, Jack watched the landscape slowly change as they travelled south-eastwards, following the curve of the River Wisla. The medieval spires of Danzig were soon left far behind. Now a desolate winter landscape stretched ahead, empty except for a few scattered farmsteads and the occasional tree, stretching bare branches towards the sky.

The day wore on. The stagecoach stopped occasionally to pick passengers up or to set others down. Wrapped snugly in his coat and scarf, Ben slumped down in his seat and closed his eyes. Filip dozed off. Emily nodded sleepily over a book. Some of the peasant women rested their chins on their chests, or their neighbour's shoulder, and fell asleep, lulled by the rocking of the coach.

Jack, however, stayed wide awake, watching the countryside roll past the window. He couldn't quite believe that they were actually here, in Poland. He just hoped that a cure awaited Ben at the end of their long journey.

Emily woke with a start. The coach had stopped! She blinked and looked around, wondering how long she'd been asleep. Several hours, she guessed, because evening was closing in. While she had dozed, someone had lit two oil lamps and fitted them into brackets on the walls of the coach.

Outside it was almost dark, but Emily could just make out a series of long low buildings with brightly-lit windows.

"What's happening?" she asked, rubbing her stiff neck. Around her, people were shuffling and standing up, gathering their belongings before filing out of the coach door.

"We stop here for the night," Filip explained. "There is a tavern where we may eat and sleep. Bartosz will wake everyone at dawn and then our journey will continue."

For the next three days Emily woke at dawn and spent her days sitting for hours on a thinly-padded bench seat, wedged between Filip and the window, helplessly watching her brother become steadily more feverish – and alarmingly thin. He ate scarcely any food at the taverns and inns where the coach stopped, although the friends tried to tempt him with tasty morsels. While his companions ate, Ben curled up by the fireplace and stared blankly at the wall. His eyes had taken on a slight milky-white glaze, which Emily recognized all too well from the lampirs she had fought.

Towards the end of each day's travel, the braziers lost their heat and a bone-numbing chill set in. Night fell quickly: a thick, impenetrable darkness pressing against the coach windows.

Once or twice Emily heard a strange sound echoing through the moonless night. "What is that?" she asked Filip.

He tilted his head for a moment, listening until the sound came again. "It's just a wolf," he said matter-of-factly.

Emily shivered. Each day as the pale winter sun began to slip towards the horizon, and the oil lamps were lit inside the coach, she began to dread the coming of night.

On the final full day of travel, Emily noticed that there were only two other passengers left on board the coach besides her own party. Bartosz had told them that this day would be the longest one of the journey and that Kornel would not call a halt until very late into the night. There would be a chance for the horses to drink, but otherwise the coach would press on until they reached Plock, their last overnight stop before Warsaw.

One of the onward-passengers was a jolly old woman in a blue-striped headscarf. Her name was Hanna, and she told Emily that she was going to visit her daughter in Warsaw. The other was a handsome man with curly chestnut hair and dark eyes who introduced himself as Olek Pilenz, a young banker en route to Krakow in the south. He and Filip talked in Polish for a while. But as sunset approached, their conversation faltered.

Night closed in. Filip lit the two oil lamps and raked through the smouldering coals in the brazier beneath Ben's feet.

"You shiver so much, my friend," he said softly, tucking his own scarf around Ben's neck.

"I'm cold all the time," Ben whispered hoarsely, his breath rasping in his throat. "And I can't see properly. My vision's going blurry. . ."

Ben soon drifted into a feverish sleep. Old Hanna dozed. Olek Pilenz stretched his legs out on to one of the empty seats, his hat over his eyes, and was soon snoring gently. None of them woke up when the stagecoach lurched to a stop.

Jack, Filip and Emily exchanged curious glances.

"Have we arrived at Plock?" Emily asked.

"Kornel said we will not reach Plock until midnight," Filip replied, consulting his pocket watch. "And it is only five-and-twenty minutes past nine."

"Perhaps this is a water stop for the horses," Jack suggested.

Emily was nearest to the window and she rubbed her cuff against the glass. It was so cold that feathery ice crystals had formed on the pane, and she had to breathe on them to clear a circle to see through.

"We're at a crossroads," she told the others. "It's very dark, and I can't see much because the road is surrounded by forest." She caught a glimpse of the night sky through the bare branches of the trees and added, "It's cloudy, but there's a bright moon tonight."

Jack came and peered over Emily's shoulder. "Bartosz is giving the horses some water," he murmured. "And Kornel's wandering off up the road. He's probably going to stretch his legs."

Jack moved away from the window, but Emily carried on watching as Bartosz finished up with the horses. Hitching up the collar of his sheepskin coat, the groom went to the side of the road to swill out one of the wooden buckets. As he turned back towards the stagecoach, Emily caught a flashing glimpse of movement as two men broke free from the shadows and began to run. . .

For a moment Emily thought they were bandits. But then she saw their deathly-white faces and claw-like hands. "Lampirs!" she cried.

CHAPTER SIX

Jack was on his feet in an instant, almost colliding with Filip as they both made a grab for one of the wall-mounted oil lamps.

"Take it, Jack," Filip said grimly. "I will seize the other."

"What can I use as a weapon?" Emily asked frantically. And Jack – who knew better than to tell her to stay in the coach – gave her his oil lamp.

"Have this," he said. "And stay close to me!"

Emily was right on Jack's heels as he leaped down from the coach. Filip was still wrestling with the bracket which held the other lamp to the wall of the coach.

The moon was partly hidden by ragged clouds which scudded across the night sky, but by the light of Emily's lamp, Jack could see that Bartosz was down. His boots scraped on the gravel as the groom desperately tried to get away from the two lampirs.

The creatures were a middle-aged man and a boy of about fifteen. Father and son, Jack thought, judging by the same thick black hair that swept back from their foreheads. They both wore the ragged remnants of sheepskin coats. The boy was thin-faced with a long nose, while the man had a bushy black beard. As the walking dead, the flesh had begun to rot from their bones. And they were making the most terrible rasping, guttural, inhuman sound: the lampir death rattle.

"*Nie!*" Bartosz shouted in Polish, his face rigid with terror. *No!*

The lampir-boy reached down, seized a handful of the groom's coat and pinned him to the ground with an inhuman strength. Bartosz whimpered as the lampir loomed over him. The boy's lips curled back from a double row of sharp fangs as he prepared to bite into the groom's flesh.

Jack ran to help Bartosz, wrenching the lampir-boy away from the groom. He looked up to see Emily let out a furious yell and leap at the other lampir. She dashed her lamp against the ragged clothes hanging from the man's body and the lamp oil slopped out on to the fabric, chased by a tiny blue flame. The clothes smouldered for a moment, then the fire caught, and the lampir-man was engulfed in a bright orange inferno which lit up the night. A horrible smell of lamp oil and burning flesh filled the air as the creature shrieked with agony. For an instant, he held his shape. Then he collapsed downwards into a pile of gritty, grey ash. The empty oil lamp lay upside down amongst the lampir's remains.

The lampir-boy saw what had happened and hissed with rage. He moved towards Jack, but at that moment, Filip leaped out of the stagecoach with the other oil lamp in his hand. He dashed past Jack towards the lampir-boy, making the creature hesitate. Before Filip could reach him, however, two more lampirs lurched out of the forest!

The first was a stocky peasant woman with muscular arms and a square jaw. A grey headscarf was bound tightly around her head and she wore a ragged grey-and-red dress with dead leaves clinging to the hem. As she approached, Jack saw that her shoes had cracked, and the splits in the leather revealed hideous black toenails.

Beside her was another lampir, a young girl in a rough-spun woollen dress. Jack glanced from the lampir-girl to the lampir-boy. They were a similar height and build, with the same thick black hair, and he realized to his horror that they must be brother and sister. Was this a family of lampirs – hiding in the forest and seeking the blood of unwary travellers?

The girl's thin, clawed hands swiped the air as she dashed towards the stagecoach. The peasant woman charged at Filip, hitting him so hard that the breath was knocked from his body. Filip grunted and let go of the oil lamp, which flew from his grasp, making a bright arc through the air.

With a desperate yelp, Jack leaped for the lamp. But

he couldn't catch it. It hit the ground with a clatter and rolled away, its flame guttering.

Immediately the peasant woman turned and lunged at Jack. But she seemed to change her mind halfway through her attack. As she drew near to Jack, she suddenly drew back, raising a brawny hand as if to ward him off. The girl and the boy lurched towards the woman who had once been their mother. Jack realized that, together, the hideous family of lampirs formed a deadly barrier between the friends and the one oil lamp that remained alight.

"We have to get that lamp before it goes out," Emily cried frantically. "It's our only weapon." She picked up a rock from the roadside and hurled it at the young girl.

The lampir-girl's attention had been on Jack, so she didn't see the rock coming. It cracked against her shoulder, and there was the sound of dry bone snapping. The lampir-creature fell backwards. Emily grabbed up another rock and leaped forwards to fight.

Jack stooped to pick up a rock of his own, while Filip darted forwards to grapple with the peasant woman. The creature lashed out at Filip with one muscular arm. But the little Polish man ducked down on to hands and knees, letting the woman's own bodyweight pitch her forward across his back.

The woman fell face down on to the gravel in front of Jack with a high-pitched shriek of rage. Instantly, her brawny hand shot out and grasped Jack's ankle tightly.

With terrifying strength, she jerked Jack's leg out from under him, so that he landed flat on his back with a yell. To his left, he could see Emily, struggling against the snarling lampir-girl. Nearby, Filip was wrestling with the black-haired boy, who was snapping his vicious fangs dangerously close to Filip's face. And the lampir-woman still had hold of Jack's ankle. . .

Clenching his teeth, Jack took aim and sent his rock flying into her ribs.

Dry dust exploded around the missile and a hideous stench filled the air. Jack gagged, but felt a rush of satisfaction. At last he had inflicted some real damage!

He took aim with his foot and kicked out at his attacker, but without warning, the lampir-woman vanished.

"Shadow-form!" yelled Filip.

Jack blinked and looked around wildly. Filip was still wrestling with the lampir-boy, but on the ground nearby, a stocky black shadow rippled and shifted like a pool of tar. It was the peasant woman – she was hidden in a shadow!

"She is using the moonlight to melt into shadow-form," Filip panted. "She knows she is safer like that. She can use surprise to her advantage, sneak up behind you, and rematerialize into human-form!" The friends had encountered this in London. Jack knew that as long as there was light of any kind, a lampir could avoid attack by becoming a shadow. In daylight, the lampirs dared not take physical shape, for the sun's light was deadly to them. But in the glow of the harmless moon, they could change from shadow to physical form, and back, at will.

"We have to get that oil lamp," Emily cried desperately, moving away from the lampir-girl and edging towards the lamp. "Or we're going to lose this fight."

The fallen lamp was still burning, although its flame was feeble now. In front of it, the lampir-woman in shadow-form dappled the gravel with black and then rematerialized. She swayed for a moment, her stocky form black against the moonlight, and then she reached for Emily.

Emily bravely lunged forwards, ducking beneath the woman's arms in a desperate attempt to reach the oil lamp.

"Watch out, Em!" Jack cried in alarm. He tried to reach her, but the lampir-girl surged up in front of him. She didn't attack immediately, but swayed from side to side, indecisively, blocking his line of sight. Jack frowned. *Why isn't the girl attacking me?* he wondered. But he didn't have time to think about it now.

He could no longer see Emily, but he heard her cry out as she struggled with the lampir-woman. Determinedly, Jack surged forwards, intending to barge the lampir-girl out of the way and help his friend. But, before he reached her, the girl simply dissolved into shadow just like her mother had done.

At last Jack could see Emily clearly. The lampir-woman had wrapped one of her powerful arms around Emily's waist and was lifting her, kicking and screaming, off the ground. With a triumphant howl, the woman thrust a clawed hand into Emily's long hair and jerked her head back. Jack saw the woman's vicious fangs gleam in the moonlight as she bared her teeth and leaned forwards to bite. And he knew he wasn't going to reach Emily in time.

CHAPTER SEVEN

Ben opened his eyes and tried to blink away the blurriness in his vision. He'd been dreaming about being outside in the snow in Bedford Square, alone, wearing just a thin shirt and breeches. He was cold. So cold! In the dream a freezing wind cut him to the bone.

But now he realized the chill in the air was real. An icy draught whistled around his ankles. Shivering, he sat up and peered around the dim interior of the coach. Where were his friends? Hanna and Olek were still there, fast asleep. But there was no sign of Emily, Jack or Filip. And the coach door was wide open. . .

He peered through the doorway and could just make out Emily. She was caught up in a desperate struggle with someone – or *something*. And despite his hazy vision, Ben knew immediately what that something was.

White face, sunken eyeballs, gleaming rows of sharp fangs: a *lampir*!

Heart pounding, Ben staggered through the door and

down the steps. The world seemed to swing as he hit the ground. Around him, blurred and indistinct, he could make out Jack and Filip, and two more lampirs – a girl and a boy. It was an ambush!

He could see that Jack and Filip were holding their own, whereas Emily was clearly in trouble. The lampir was lifting her off the ground, and as Ben stumbled towards his sister, he realized that it was preparing to bite.

Staggering forwards, Ben seized the lampir's ragged clothes and hauled it away from his sister. He registered briefly that the creature was a woman. She was wearing a headscarf which had slipped to reveal long strands of grey hair.

Taken by surprise, the lampir-woman dropped Emily and twisted round to attack Ben, her fangs bared in a hungry leer, ready to bite. But as she looked into his face, the lampir-woman hesitated. For a moment, Ben was confused. Then he realized that the lampir must have recognized that he was infected with the plague!

Over the woman's shoulder, Ben saw Emily scramble back to the coach and clamber up to the driver's seat.

What is she doing? he thought. And then Ben saw that there was another oil lamp suspended from a hook above Kornel's seat. The wick had been turned down low, so only a small flame was visible through the smoky glass. But it was enough. Emily lifted the lamp carefully, jumped back down to the ground, and smashed the lamp over the lampir-woman's shoulders as she stood staring uncertainly at Ben.

The lampir-woman immediately burst into flames. Her headscarf and the strands of grey hair caught fire easily, crackling like fireworks. Orange and red flames flared up so brightly that Ben could feel the heat on his face.

Jack gave a yell of triumph, and Ben watched as he and Filip together shoved the boy-lampir into the flames. Both lampirs burned quickly and then crumbled into ash.

The last lampir – the young girl – howled and gnashed her fangs. She reached out to grab Jack, opened her mouth to bite him, and then changed her mind and pushed him away with a frustrated screech. With her breath rasping in her throat, the lampir-girl staggered backwards, then turned and ran for the trees.

Filip darted forwards and snatched up the lamp that he had dropped earlier. Running to the side of the road, he hurled it after the girl. It struck her squarely in the centre of her back, and the rough woollen dress caught fire immediately. Bright flames flickered hungrily around the lampir as she stumbled into the forest.

"You don't get away that easily," Filip said grimly, as he watched the lampir-girl finally disintegrate.

Ben glanced around quickly, and realized with relief that all the lampirs had been defeated. But his attention was caught by the serious expression in Filip's eyes. He had seized hold of Jack and was tilting the boy's face up to the moonlight.

"Why did those lampirs back away from you, Jack?" Filip demanded. "Ben is infected – the creatures recognized that. They can always tell when they are faced with one of their own. But you, my friend. . . ?"

Ben watched as Emily hurried over to examine Jack too. Her hair was tangled and there was a rip in the bodice of her gown, but otherwise she looked unharmed. But the thought that his best friend might be infected with lampir plague too made Ben's legs go weak. He sat down abruptly on a nearby tree stump.

Filip and Emily continued to examine Jack. They pulled back his cuffs to inspect his wrists and then peered closely at his neck.

"There's not a scratch on him," Emily muttered at last.

Jack nodded, checking his hands carefully, even peering beneath the heavy gold ring on his finger. "The only close contact I had with a lampir was when the peasant woman grabbed my ankle," he said at last, and leaned down to check his lower legs and feet. But they were completely unscathed.

"It is a mystery," Filip said at last. "Why did the lampir-girl suddenly decide to flee like that?"

Emily bit her lip. "Maybe Jack *was* infected just now, and the creature sensed it," she said thoughtfully. "But with all the lampirs now dead, we've killed the lampir that infected him. So Jack has been cured instantly."

Filip nodded slowly. "That is a sensible theory, Emily."

Jack nodded too. Then he glanced across at Ben and let out a muttered curse when he saw his friend slumped on the tree trunk. "Ben, me old mate. You all right?"

Ben nodded as they all hurried over to him. "Exhausted," he muttered. "But I'll live – for now. Poor Bartosz doesn't look in terribly good shape, though."

The groom was still huddled on the ground, his sheepskin coat ripped open. But he was stirring, and Filip hurried to help him up. "Take it slowly, Bartosz," he said gently.

"*Co sie stalo?*" the poor man asked with a groan. *What happened?*

But before anyone could answer, another noise echoed through the chill night air: the sound of heavy footsteps crunching on snowy gravel.

Straining his eyes to peer into the darkness, Ben felt Emily's hand grip his sleeve nervously. Could it be that more lampirs were coming?

CHAPTER EIGHT

Jack held his breath as a dark figure emerged from the shadows. Tall and broad-shouldered, it was a man who trudged along the road towards them with a heavy tread. Then Jack recognized the sheepskin coat and baggy trousers. "It's Kornel – the driver!" Jack cried, almost laughing with relief.

"Where on earth has he been?" Emily muttered.

Kornel saw them all standing outside the coach and gave a cheery wave as he approached. "I have food!" he exclaimed in heavily-accented English, brandishing a bulging hessian bag. "I am visiting my Aunt Eva who is living near here. . ." His voice tailed off as he took in the smashed lamps, and Bartosz's dishevelled appearance. "What happened?"

Bartosz was now sitting up, rubbing his forehead. He spoke quickly to Kornel in Polish, his words tumbling over each other and his voice high-pitched with panic. Jack guessed that he was explaining how the coach had been attacked. He caught the word "lampirs" several times.

Kornel listened, his face registering shock, then horror, then utter disbelief. At last he threw his head back and laughed. "Since when have you believed in folktales like that, Bartosz?" he demanded, smiling, and Filip translated his scornful words for the others.

Bartosz scrambled to his feet. "Never before tonight!" he cried. "I did not take the old stories seriously. But how can I doubt my own eyes?" He held his hand up, finger and thumb just an inch apart. "I was *this* close to a lampir, Kornel. I smelled its breath upon my face. And it stank of death!"

"And no doubt if I smelled *your* breath, old friend, it would stink of brandy," Kornel said dismissively. "They were probably just bandits."

"I am not drunk!" insisted Bartosz. "I know what I saw."

Jack stepped forward. "If it was bandits," he said reasonably to Kornel. "Why ain't they stolen anything?"

Kornel shrugged. "You all put up a good fight and scared them away," he suggested.

Filip sighed. "Don't be so quick to dismiss Bartosz's story," he said quietly. "You would do well to take care when you are on the road after dark."

Kornel turned to Filip and patted him on the back. "Sure, sure," he said, chuckling. "Now, all aboard, my friends. We move on!"

Jack and Emily went to help Ben back into the coach. He was shivering and weak. Behind them Filip spoke quietly in Polish to Kornel and Bartosz.

Inside, Hanna and Olek had both woken up. Olek was sitting in the far corner rubbing his eyes sleepily. But Hanna was on her knees, hands folded in prayer. A silver crucifix on a chain dangled from between her fingers, and she was muttering softly.

Emily nudged Jack. "Looks like Hanna saw part of the attack," she murmured.

As Jack helped Ben, Emily gently touched Hanna's shoulder.

The old woman opened her eyes. Her strongly-accented voice rose in terror as she said, "The lampir. . ." She pronounced it *hlompeeer*. "There are so many now. More and more, they come."

But Olek smiled, turning up his collar against the cold. "I apologize on behalf of my fellow Poles," he said. "Folk seem to be getting more and more superstitious of late. There is a plague spreading across my land, and *some* people think that it is caused by a mythical creature called a lampir. But this is, of course, nothing but an old wives' tale."

Filip stepped up into the carriage just then. He obviously heard Olek's words, because he exchanged an exasperated glance with Jack. "Olek is exactly like Kornel," he murmured to Jack. "Some people refuse to accept the truth – even when the evidence is right before them."

And that, Jack thought, as the stagecoach rocked into motion and began to creak forward into the night, *seems to sum up the Polish*. Some, like Hanna and Filip, knew the truth about lampir plague. Others refused to accept the evidence of their own eyes, and insisted that people who believed in lampirs were utter fools.

As he settled down to sleep, Jack thought he knew who the greater fools were.

It was nearly midnight when they reached an inn in the town of Plock. The small and subdued band of weary travellers warmed their hands before the fire, while the inn-keeper bustled about wrapping hot bricks in flannel to warm the beds. Jack, Ben and Filip shared a room, and it felt to Jack as if he had only just settled his head on the pillow and closed his eyes, when a hand was shaking him awake again.

But it was dawn, cold and clear. Kornel was in the inn-yard, harnessing fresh horses to the stagecoach. Bartosz looked bright and cheerful, last night's attack forgotten in the light of day.

Throughout the morning, Jack sat with his nose pressed to the coach window. Under a grey sky, the flat, frozen landscape slipped past. Soon he caught glimpses of a wide river snaking its way through the countryside. Filip told him that it was the Wisla, the longest river in Poland, and that the city of Warsaw had been built around it, beginning as a small fishing village but now populated by almost two hundred thousand people.

Jack turned to Emily. "We must be nearly there," he said.

Emily was sitting opposite Jack, her shoulder tucked against Ben's. But now she leaned forwards too, eager to catch a glimpse of their destination.

The sun came out just as Jack spotted a mass of snow-capped city buildings in the far distance. He could just make out high, red stone walls, towers and turrets, and gleaming golden gates. The pale silvery rays of winter sunshine glittered from the tips of tall church spires. He nudged Filip, who had been dozing, and pointed a finger.

Filip blinked once or twice, rubbed the sleep from his eyes, and peered past Jack's shoulder. A jubilant grin spread across his bony features. "Ah, yes," he said, bursting with pride. "That, my young friend, is the city of Warsaw itself. My home!"

CHAPTER NINE

WARSAW, JANUARY 1851

The three friends and Filip left the stagecoach at a coaching inn on the outskirts of the city, and hired a four-seater "Berlin" carriage to take them to Filip's house. The Berlin bowled southwards through the Old Town, carrying the little party of travellers along wide boulevards lined with grand monuments and colourful terraced houses, painted in pink and apricot and duck-egg blue. People hurried this way and that, muffled against the cold in fur hats and coats.

Emily felt a thrill of excitement as she gazed out of the window, drinking in the scenery. Soft snow cloaked rooftops, lamp-posts and pavements, while ice crystals glittered in the late-morning sunshine. Warsaw looked like a fairytale city.

"Look," said Filip, pointing. "Between these buildings you will catch glimpses of the River Wisla. See the water dotted with boats and barges? And now we have arrived at my home!"

The Berlin carriage had come to the end of a long cobbled street and stopped before a row of well-kept three-storey townhouses, all of them painted a buttermilk yellow. One of them had a glossy, dark-blue front door. Alongside it was a bell-pull and a gleaming brass plaque which read, *Doktor Roman Cinska*.

Filip paid the Berlin driver and fished a key out of his waistcoat pocket, as Emily and Jack helped Ben out of the carriage. He stumbled a little and Emily looped her arm through his, hoping that they would find a cure for him now that they had reached the end of their journey.

Soon they were inside the wide, bright hallway with a pile of luggage at their feet, marvelling at the warmth after the freezing temperatures outside. The house smelled of lemons and beeswax furniture polish. Against one custard-yellow wall was a row of wooden chairs, and Emily gently steered Ben towards them.

"Sit down," she said softly, and Ben immediately sank down on to one of them with a look of profound relief.

Emily looked around at her new surroundings with interest. On her right, a narrow staircase rose to the upper floors. At the bottom of the stairs, an open door led into a study, which was obviously used as Doctor Roman Cinska's consulting room. The pale-green walls were lined with bookshelves and little glass cupboards full of pill jars and brown bottles.

Emily heard hurried footsteps approaching up a set of basement stairs at the rear of the hall, and a man emerged, muttering to himself. Tall and lean, with smooth blond hair streaked grey at the temples, he had a long bony nose and serious blue eyes. A pair of round spectacles dangled around his neck on a thin black cord.

"Roman!" cried Filip, dashing forwards to greet the man.

So this is Roman Cinska, Emily thought, studying him curiously. Neatly dressed in grey flannel trousers, waistcoat, and silver cravat, the doctor was very different to his brother Filip, who always looked rather dishevelled.

"Filip!" Roman grasped Filip by the shoulder and chattered away happily to him in Polish.

Filip laughed. "No, no, speak English, brother," he said, gesturing towards Jack, Ben and Emily. "My friends do not speak our language."

Roman turned to the friends and gave them a broad smile. "I've just made a very exciting breakthrough in the development of my serum!" he told them eagerly. "Quite by chance I have discovered that stirring just five granules of Allium Sativum into the mixture creates a rather spectacular reaction. I want to make notes about the experiment, but I can't find my spectacles!"

Filip chuckled. "They're right in front of your nose," he said, pointing out the spectacles on their length of black cord.

"Ah, so they are." Roman seized the spectacles and began to polish them with a large white handkerchief. "Now, where was I?"

But Filip broke in, grinning. "What, no 'Welcome home, brother'? I see it has escaped your notice that I've been absent from the house for almost a month!"

Roman pulled himself up, laughing. "Of course! Forgive me, Filip. Welcome home. I trust you enjoyed your trip?"

"Enjoyed is not a word I would use," Filip admitted. "But it has been useful." He patted the blue hat-box. "I managed to retrieve the Dhampir Bell."

Still cleaning his little round spectacles, Roman rolled his eyes towards the heavens. "You and your bell," he said good-humouredly. "A lot of superstitious nonsense. When will you accept that an old bronze bell has no more power over the plague that afflicts this city than ... than ... *my spectacles*? Science is our only hope, brother." He chuckled as he glanced at Filip. "Science, and modern medicine."

Filip shrugged. "I hope you're right," he said gently. "But so far science has failed us."

Roman finished polishing his spectacles and jammed them on to the bridge of his bony nose. Then he turned to the three friends just inside the door. "But you've guests, brother!" he exclaimed, stuffing his handkerchief back into his trouser pocket. "Please, introduce them to me."

Filip duly introduced them, one by one. "This is Miss Emily Cole, from England." Emily smiled as the courteous doctor bowed low over her hand.

"And my young friend, Jack Harkett." Roman shook Jack's hand.

"And this is Miss Emily's brother, Benedict Cole."

"Good morning," Roman said, gazing down at Ben, who was still slumped in one of the chairs. "You are not well, I see."

Crouching down, Roman gently took Ben's wrist between his thumb and forefinger, feeling for the pulse which would reflect Ben's heartbeat. He shook his head. "Slow. Too slow."

"He has lampir plague," Emily explained simply.

Roman shook his head, not taking his eyes off Ben. "Your brother has indeed contracted a form of plague, Miss Emily. But there are no such things as lampirs. You should not listen to my brother and his old wives' tales."

Emily bit her lip. She was tempted to tell Roman that she'd seen lampirs with her own eyes – many times. But she knew that they needed Roman on their side, and arguing wouldn't help.

She watched as the doctor spoke kindly to Ben, asking him to open his mouth wide and say "Aaah". Then the doctor proceeded to feel gently along Ben's jaw with the tips of his fingers.

At last Roman Cinska stood up. He took his spectacles off and began to polish them again. "The stage of your brother's illness is quite advanced, Miss Emily. Do you know when he was infected?"

"Yes," Emily said. "It was Christmas Day. Ben was scratched by a plague victim's fingernail." She didn't mention that the fingernail had been on a severed hand, because it was obvious that sceptical Roman wouldn't believe her.

"A scratch from a fingernail, you say? That is very interesting and accords with some of my recent research." Frowning, Roman put his spectacles back on and studied Ben for a moment. "And you say this scratch occurred on Christmas Day?"

Emily nodded. She could see the doctor was rapidly calculating in his head. His expression became very grim. "There is not much time," he said. "This plague is usually fatal within twenty-one days, and already more than half that time has passed. This boy needs urgent help."

Ben struggled to sit upright. "The serum," he whispered hoarsely. "You said you had just made an exciting breakthrough. . ."

But Roman shook his head. "Indeed I have. But the serum is merely at the experimental phase. It will be many days before it is ready for use on humans – perhaps weeks."

"But we don't have weeks," Jack pointed out. "Ben needs the serum now."

Again Roman shook his head. "I am sorry. I would

like to help your young friend. But it would be highly dangerous to inject a human being with an untested chemical formula."

"But we've travelled hundreds of miles to seek your help," Emily argued. "Please, Doctor Cinska. Your serum is Ben's only hope."

"It could kill him," Roman pointed out.

Emily swallowed hard and reached for Ben's hand. "He's going to die anyway. We've nothing to lose," she said flatly. "And if the serum works, you will have found the key to stopping this plague in its tracks."

Roman adjusted his spectacles, staring thoughtfully at Ben's chalk-white face. "I am afraid you are right," he said at last. "And heaven knows this plague needs to be stopped. I had six patients waiting at my front door this morning. Six!" He glanced at Filip. "Not long after you left for England, brother, a fresh outbreak of this plague hit Warsaw. I have never been so busy. My house calls take me most of the day, and I work on my serum all evening."

Roman ran his hands through his tidy blond hair, tousling it, and for an instant Emily could see how alike the brothers really were.

"How soon after I left did the outbreak begin?" Filip enquired.

"About ten days or so – why do you ask?" Roman replied.

"Ten days. . ." Filip exchanged a glance with Jack and

Emily. "That would be about the time that Sir Peter Walker rang the Dhampir Bell. You remember, brother, that I told you the chime of the bell would free the trapped lampirs from their graves? Well, the chime did indeed wake the undead in London. And by the sound of it, here in Poland too." He patted the hat-box and added, "My task now is to find out how the Dhampir Bell can be used to recapture these lampirs—"

"And end the plague that stalks our streets. . . Yes, yes!" Roman finished Filip's sentence with a snort of laughter. "A leopard never changes its spots, and neither do you, my dear brother." He sighed. "As always, the argument between us is science versus superstition!"

Emily stepped forwards and placed her hand on Roman's arm. "Please don't argue with each other," she said. "At this moment my brother is dying. If you want to prove that science is more effective than superstition, then please, use the serum."

Ben sank back against the cushion Roman had placed beneath his head. He was so bone-weary now that he didn't care if he never got up again. He was lying on a leather couch in the basement of the Cinska residence, which the doctor had obviously set up as his laboratory. Against one of the whitewashed brick walls stood a desk, its surface covered with pages of notes, and neat piles of Roman's papers and journals. Along the opposite wall stood a long, wooden workbench where a spirit lamp burned brightly beneath a metal tripod. The shelf above was piled high with scientific apparatus: coils of copper wire, lengths of brown rubber tubing, thermometers, wooden tongs, and several racks of thin glass tubes. High in one wall was a single, grimy window which let in a thin shaft of dusty light.

Emily, Jack and Filip hovered around Ben, looking concerned. Roman rolled up his shirtsleeves and went across to the workbench. He lit the flame on the spirit lamp and set a balloon-shaped glass beaker of clear liquid over it to heat. Soon the liquid began to froth and hiss.

"As Filip has probably told you, for many years I have been trying to discover a medicine which will cure this dreadful plague," Roman explained. "I have the basic formula here in this beaker." He lifted the balloon-shaped beaker off the heat and reached for a small glass phial. "I pour a small amount into this phial, which we scientists call a test tube. Then I add exactly five granules of dried Allium Sativum, like this. . ." He put the balloon-shaped beaker back over the heat and then carefully added five yellow crystals to the test tube.

"Before this morning, I had not used this particular ingredient. But look. . ." Roman said, as he stirred the mixture using a long, thin silver rod.

Ben watched as the liquid in the test tube fizzed slightly. Then it turned a bright, acid green and emitted a puff of smoky, sulphurous vapour. He could see that

71

the others looked fascinated, but Ben could barely summon up the strength to keep his eyes open.

"It smells horrible," Emily muttered, waving her hand in front of her nose.

Roman turned to the friends, holding up the test tube. "As you see, after a few moments the serum settles to become a clear liquid once again," he said, as behind him the mixture in the balloon-shaped glass beaker frothed and hissed over the spirit lamp. "It is this which I hope will prove to be the antidote to the plague. But to test whether my theory works, I need a fresh drop of blood from an infected person. With your permission, Benedict, I will prick the tip of your finger. . ."

Ben nodded wearily. He felt so terrible that he didn't care what Roman did to him.

"I also need an extra pair of hands to assist me." Roman glanced at Emily. "Miss Emily, would you be so kind?"

Ben watched blurrily as Roman and Emily crouched beside the couch. He could barely see them through the mist that had formed in front of his eyes, and their soft voices seemed indistinct, as if they were far away rather than kneeling right next to him. He felt a sharp pain in his finger, and then pressure as Roman squeezed firmly.

Ben could just make out the gleaming droplet of dusky purple blood which had formed like a shiny bead on his fingertip.

"Is blood usually that colour?" asked Emily doubtfully.

Roman shook his head. "Healthy human blood is red," he replied. "But always with this plague, the sufferer's blood turns purple, just like their nails."

The droplet of Ben's blood hung on the tip of his finger for a moment, poised. Then it dropped into the test tube where it floated on top of the serum like a round, purple berry. Emily handed the tube carefully back to Roman.

For a moment, nothing happened. Then the serum began to fizz up into a thousand tiny bubbles. Despite his hazy vision, Ben could see that the droplet of his blood was quickly changing colour, from dusky purple to livid indigo. For a moment it shimmered through a kaleidoscope of colours – mauve, violet and lurid pink – before it finally settled to a bright, healthy-looking red.

Then, abruptly, it sank to the bottom of the test tube.

Jack felt his hopes for Ben's recovery plummet with the drop of blood. "What's happened?" he asked anxiously.

Roman straightened, holding the glass phial up to the light. For a moment he said nothing, and frowned in concentration. Then he smiled and patted Jack's shoulder. "What has happened? Why, your young friend's blood has just returned to normal," he declared. "The serum has changed the composition of Benedict's blood, from plague-infected to healthy. And I know from past experiments that a droplet of healthy blood will sink, because it is thicker and heavier than the serum, while infected blood is not."

The doctor placed the test tube into a rack on the workbench. He removed his spectacles and turned to look at Ben, his expression grave. "So, Benedict. You have seen the dramatic effect that my serum has on a mere droplet of blood. Imagine that effect magnified a hundred-fold when the serum is injected into the human body. There is no guarantee that it will cure you. Indeed, it may even kill you. Are you sure that you wish to proceed with such an experimental treatment?"

At the thought of the serum fizzing through Ben's veins, Jack's heart began to pound. He saw Emily bite her lip worriedly. *Are we doing the right thing?* he wondered. But he knew in his heart that this really was Ben's last hope. And he was sure that Emily realized that, too.

Over on the couch, Ben was nodding weakly. "Please. . ." he croaked. "Just do it."

Roman nodded and put his spectacles back on. "Filip," he said to his brother. "Why don't you take Jack and Miss Emily upstairs and ask the housekeeper to brew some tea? These young people must be in need of refreshment after their long journey – and I am in need of a little space to prepare my equipment."

Jack and Emily wished Ben luck and then followed Filip, who was muttering about delicious Polish tea. As they left the laboratory, Emily glanced back over her shoulder. Her face was pale and tense, and Jack knew she was probably thinking exactly the same thing he was: *Will this be the last time I ever see Ben alive?*

CHAPTER TEN

Ben closed his eyes and listened to the chink of metal and the tinkle of glass as Roman prepared the injection. He could smell the serum bubbling in the balloon-shaped beaker over the spirit lamp. Then the doctor was at his side, speaking in a gentle, reassuring voice.

"Just a little sharp sensation. . . So!" the doctor said. "And you may feel a little cold in your arm as I inject the serum into your vein."

"It is cold," Ben admitted. He could feel the serum coursing through his veins as it spread from his arm to the rest of his body. "But it feels nice – kind of fizzy."

He opened his eyes. Was his vision a little less blurry already?

Roman smiled at him and withdrew the needle. "I will just press a cotton pad against the puncture for a moment, in case of any bleeding. How do you feel?"

But before Ben could reply, the serum that had been simmering over the spirit lamp began to overheat. Ben could see it frothing wildly. "Roman!" he cried, pointing.

But it was too late. Even as the doctor glanced back over his shoulder, the glass beaker exploded, sending a spray of hot serum and shattered glass flying across the laboratory.

Roman gave a startled cry and flung himself forwards over the couch, bravely shielding Ben with his body. For a moment, the room was full of the tinkling sound of glass hitting the stone floor and the hiss of the spirit lamp. Then there was silence.

After a moment, Roman straightened up and adjusted his spectacles. "Are you all right, Benedict?" he asked.

Ben sat up gingerly. "I'm fine, thank you. But *you* aren't!"

Roman followed the line of Ben's gaze and cursed softly. Several needle-sharp shards of glass from the exploded beaker had embedded themselves in his bare forearm. Blood trickled from one of the cuts.

Just then footsteps pounded down the basement steps, and the door flew open as Jack, Emily and Filip burst into the laboratory. Ben realized that he could see their faces clearly for the first time in days, and all three looked anxious.

"We heard an explosion from upstairs!" Filip cried. "What happened?"

"I was careless, is what happened," Roman said, clearly annoyed with himself. "I was so absorbed in making the serum that I forgot the most basic rule of the laboratory: never leave a mixture unattended over a flame! But the important thing is that I have injected Ben with the serum, and it appears to be working."

Ben grinned as Jack and Emily hurried towards him. "I can feel the serum fizzing through my veins," he told them, flexing his hands.

"Does it hurt?" Emily asked.

"No, it's quite pleasant – like when you drink lime sherbet, and the bubbles go up your nose!"

Jack was peering at him. "Your eyes are looking better already, mate," he said. "Not so milky as before."

Ben rested while the others set about putting the laboratory to rights, carefully sweeping up the pieces of glass while Roman mopped up the spilt serum. Emily wrapped a bandage around the doctor's injured forearm, then Filip summoned them all upstairs for some of Florentyna the housekeeper's Polish tea and pastries.

Despite her exotic-sounding name, Florentyna turned out to be a wizened little old lady with a face like a wrinkled apple. She came to the Cinska residence for a few hours every morning to cook, clean and make beds. She spoke no English, but muttered to herself in Polish as she shuffled around the drawing room, the hem of her long black dress sweeping the carpet.

Ben felt a little apprehensive about drinking the Polish tea. He remembered the tea Filip had brewed for them in London; it had been unbelievably strong and rather overpowering. However, Florentyna's tea, which

Ben sipped cautiously, turned out to be very drinkable, and Ben swallowed it gratefully, feeling the hot liquid imparting some welcome warmth to his aching body.

As the others ate and drank, Ben paced up and down experimentally. Although his body felt bruised, and his legs were still weak, he decided that he felt better with every step he took.

Eventually he turned to the others. "I don't know about anyone else, but I'm ready to go and find Uncle Edwin at the Hotel Syrena!" he declared with a grin.

The hotel was a carriage-ride away in Castle Square, just inside the southern section of Warsaw's medieval city walls. Wide and airy, the square was a sweeping curve, paved with pink cobbles and surrounded by three- and four-storey buildings painted in dramatic tones of yellow, green, orange and sky-blue. In the centre, Ben noticed an imposing creamy-white column which towered high above the snow-capped rooftops. There was something on the top, but although he pressed his nose to the carriage window he couldn't quite make out what it was.

Jack was peering up at it too. Suddenly he said, "Blimey, there's a bronze fellow sitting on top of that pillar, with a cross in one hand and a sword in the other!"

Filip smiled. "That bronze *fellow*, as you put it, young Jack, is King Zygmunt the Third," he explained. "Ruler of Poland in the sixteenth century, and the man who made Warsaw our capital city. That castle you see on the far side of the square was his royal residence."

All three of them turned to peer out of the window at the castle. Like so many buildings in Warsaw it was fashioned in reddish-orange brick, and had a tiled roof and several towers topped with green onion-shaped domes. Just beyond it was a smaller but no less majestic-looking building. Two doormen stood outside, the silver braid on their uniforms sparkling in the pale winter sunshine.

The carriage pulled up outside the building.

"This is the Hotel Syrena," Filip declared, as one of the doormen hurried to open the door for them. "We have arrived!"

"Looks like every eminent scientist in the world has arrived along with us!" Ben said, as they hurried up the wide marble steps and entered the bustling hotel foyer. "They must all have come for the symposium, like Uncle Edwin."

Inside the hotel a throng of gentlemen in frock coats crowded around the reception desk, chattering in a dozen different languages. Bell-boys in pale blue jackets darted here and there, while porters heaved luggage towards the huge marble staircase which swept up to the higher floors.

The reception desk was a long counter of gleaming mahogany wood, manned by a clerk in a smart black coat. Filip spoke rapidly to him in Polish and a bell-boy was despatched to find Edwin Sherwood.

"Please wait in the lounge," the clerk said in English, pointing to an archway.

Ben led the others through to the lounge, where blue velvet armchairs had been grouped around little gilded tables. Graceful palm trees stood in large urns beneath oil paintings of old Warsaw.

Ben sat down gratefully in one of the armchairs – he still felt quite weak from his illness – while Jack, Emily and Filip sauntered over to look at the paintings.

They didn't have long to wait. Within a few minutes a tall, thin man with greying hair descended the marble stairs and began threading his way towards them through the crowded foyer. He was wearing a tailcoat and elegant breeches, and his skin was slightly tanned as though he'd spent several months in a hot climate.

Ben's heart leaped with joy. "Uncle Edwin!" he cried, standing up and hurrying forward to meet his godfather.

Edwin Sherwood grinned and pulled Ben into a hug. "Good to see you, my boy," he said warmly. "And here's Emily and Jack, too!"

"And this is our friend, Mr Filip Cinska," Ben put in, and Edwin leaned across one of the little gilded tables to shake Filip's hand.

"What a delightful surprise," Edwin said with a smile, making himself comfortable in one of the armchairs. "I only received your telegraph this morning, so you can imagine my astonishment when the bell-boy knocked at my door and told me that you were here already! I must admit, I'm a little anxious about finding rooms for you all at such short notice. The Syrena is fully booked with delegates to the symposium." He frowned thoughtfully and added, "I suppose you could share my room. It's quite small, but there's a couch and—"

"I will not hear of such a thing!" Filip interrupted with a quick shake of his head. "My brother and I would be horrified to think of anybody sleeping on a couch when there are spare beds in our house."

"Are you sure?" Ben asked.

"I will be offended if you refuse!" Filip declared, his eyes twinkling.

"Then that's settled," Edwin said and smiled. "Now, tell me how you've all been keeping. Jack, Emily, you're both looking well. But Ben – I almost didn't recognize you! You're as thin as a rake. What's happened to you?"

There was a small silence as everyone looked at Ben.

"Oh, it's nothing," he said casually. He felt that there was no point in mentioning lampir plague and worrying Uncle Edwin when he was so busy with the symposium. There would be time enough to share their news when all the important speeches were over. "I stayed out in the snow too long on Christmas Day, caught a bit of a winter chill and it put me off my food for a week or so. But I'm much better now."

"Well on the road to recovery!" Emily put in heartily.

"Yup," Jack added with a grin. "Back to his old self. Eating like a horse. You'd better watch out, Filip, or you might regret inviting Ben to stay with you. The cupboards will soon be bare!"

Filip smiled. "Ben is welcome to eat as much as he wants. As are the rest of you. Mr Sherwood, I would like to invite you to join us for a small dinner party at my house tonight, if your work schedule allows."

"I'd be delighted to accept," Edwin replied happily. He leaned forward and smiled regretfully at Ben, Emily and Jack. "I'm afraid I shan't have as much time to spend with you all as I would like. The symposium starts the day after tomorrow and I've been asked to chair the opening discussion – and to speak at an evening lecture alongside the leading Egyptologist, Sir Bracewell Smythe. And then, of course, there's my key speech on the final day. . ."

"That's all right," Emily said. "There's plenty to occupy us here. Warsaw has so many ancient monuments and such interesting architecture."

"Good, good." Edwin glanced up as a bell-boy approached and handed him a slip of paper. "Oh, dear," he said, as he read the message. "Duty calls. I'm being summoned to an emergency meeting with the organizers of the symposium. They need me to replace a speaker at rather short notice. One of our historians is unable to attend, after all. It's Sir Peter Walker – you remember him, don't you, Ben and Emily?"

Ben glanced at his sister and grinned. "Er, yes, we do!" he replied.

Edwin shook his head sadly. "Poor fellow. Apparently he's gone mad."

"Mad?" Ben queried, eyebrows raised.

Edwin nodded. "I've heard he's taken to riding around Windsor on horseback, waving a banner and shouting about having to burn corpses so the dead can't walk!"

Ben didn't dare look at the others. "Imagine that!" he said faintly.

Early the next morning, Jack awoke to bright winter sunshine. He blinked up at the ceiling, wondering for a moment what had disturbed him. Then a frantic hammering sounded on the bedroom door.

Across the room, Ben's tousled head appeared from beneath an enormous pile of blankets and quilts. "What's going on. . . ?" he asked blearily.

The next moment the door flew open and Emily appeared. "Hurry up and get dressed and come downstairs!" she cried. "Roman needs our help." And then she was gone again in a flurry of pink petticoats. They could hear her footsteps pattering down the stairs.

"Better go and see what's happening," Jack muttered, throwing back the covers and pulling on his clothes.

They could all have done with another hour of sleep, Jack reflected, as he quickly splashed cold water on his face from a china bowl on the dresser. The dinner party last night had gone on until past midnight. Edwin and Roman had sipped wine and good-naturedly wrangled over obscure points of scientific theory, while Jack, Ben, Emily and Filip had quietly celebrated Ben's good health – although, of course, Edwin Sherwood knew nothing about his godson's narrow escape from lampir plague.

Now Ben was first to the bedroom door. "Come on," he said, buttoning his jacket with one hand and smoothing his fair hair with the other. "Let's go and ask Em what's going on."

But as soon as the two boys reached the foot of the stairs they could see for themselves. . .

The hallway was crowded with people. Some of them sat on the row of chairs outside Roman's consulting room. Others crouched on the floor. The front door was open, and Jack could see more people thronging the steps and the snowy pavement beyond. Thirty or forty people were waiting to see Roman Cinska.

And Jack saw that they all had one thing in common – chalk-white faces, black-rimmed eyes and purple fingernails: lampir plague!

Almost overnight, the outbreak in Warsaw had become an epidemic.

CHAPTER ELEVEN

Roman came to the doorway of his consulting room and caught sight of Jack and Ben at the bottom of the stairs.

"Do you know how to use a mortar and pestle?" he asked hopefully, taking his spectacles off and pinching the bridge of his nose between thumb and forefinger. "All these people are waiting for a dose of serum and I have run out. I need someone to grind a batch of Allium Sativum into coarse powder."

"I can do that," Ben volunteered.

"Come then." Roman beckoned him in. "I am going to give as many doses as I can here, and then I shall take some with me when I go out on my house calls. I wonder whether you would accompany me, Benedict? If you are up to it, of course. You see, people are often afraid of new medicine, but I think they will be reassured when they hear that you have received the serum and recovered fully from the plague."

"Of course," Ben said eagerly, and he followed the doctor into his consulting room.

Jack felt a hand on his shoulder and turned to see that Filip and Emily had joined him.

Filip was gazing at the throng of sick patients, his expression grim. "My brother's medicine is a great breakthrough in our fight against lampirism," Filip murmured. "But even so, Roman's serum cannot cure the lampirs already in existence. For that we need more than medicine. We need the lost incantation that the dhampirs used with the bell, to lock the lampirs in their graves. And while my brother carries on his good work, I must dedicate myself to finding that."

"Any ideas on where to start looking?" Emily asked.

Filip nodded. "I want to visit the monastery where Sir Peter Walker first found the bell."

Jack glanced at Emily. "We'll come with you," he said, reaching for his coat.

The Monastery of St Wenceslaus was a carriage-ride away on the outskirts of Warsaw. The sprawling red-stone complex had been built into the old city walls. Medieval ramparts and watchtowers brooded over Emily, Jack and Filip as they climbed down from the Berlin.

"How are we going to get in?" asked Emily, as they gazed up at a pair of enormous, heavy oak doors.

Filip smiled. "A monastery door is like any other

door," he said simply. "We knock!" And he pounded on the heavy oak panels with his fist.

Almost immediately a small metal grille in the centre of one of the doors slid open. A red nose and a pair of merry blue eyes appeared. *"Tak?"*

Filip replied in Polish, gesturing once or twice towards Emily and Jack, and Emily realized he was explaining who they were and how far they had travelled. At last there was a clanking of keys and a rattling of bolts, and one side of the oak door creaked open to reveal a monk dressed in threadbare, rust-coloured robes and a brown cloak. He was young, probably only a year or two older than Emily herself, with rosy cheeks and a thatch of ginger hair that had been shaved into a traditional monk's tonsure around the crown of his pale-pink head.

"Friends from England, I welcome you to the house of St Wenceslaus," said the young monk cheerfully, in strongly-accented English. "My name is Brother Lubek and I shall be most pleased to take you to our abbot, Father Zachariasz."

Brother Lubek led them across an open courtyard where a few hens pecked at the dusty cobbles. The monastery buildings towered around them, throwing everything into shadow. Emily could tell by the profusion of carved angels and gargoyles that the house of St Wenceslaus had once been prosperous, even rich. But now the place had an air of faded neglect. Tiles were missing from the rooftops, the gardens were straggly and overgrown, and a silver cross on top of one of the green onion-domes was tarnished and dull.

"This way, please," Brother Lubek said, beckoning them up some worn steps and through a doorway. "In here is our hospital wing, where we monks are tending the sick and lame of our city. Sadly, many are sick at this time!"

The hospital wing was a long, low-ceilinged chamber which smelled of camphor and cloves. Fires crackled and flared at both ends of the room, making the air as hot and dry as a furnace. Emily immediately felt sweat breaking out across her forehead, and loosened her woollen scarf as she walked through the room.

The sick lay on flat wooden pallets, tended by monks who wore sackcloth aprons over their rust-coloured robes. Somewhere a child coughed, and Emily noticed an old man with a milky-white film over his eyeballs.

These people are all suffering from lampir plague, too, she thought in dismay.

Father Zachariasz was at the far end of the room overseeing a young monk who was stirring something in a huge copper pot in the fireplace. The abbot's light, quick voice lilted rapidly through a sentence in Polish.

When Emily raised her eyebrows at Filip, he translated. "The abbot is telling the young monk to try adding a handful of shredded willow bark," Filip explained. "He says it may not cure the sickness, but at least it will dull the aching of their limbs."

Father Zachariasz glanced up at the sound of Filip's voice, and Emily saw that he was a bright-eyed little man, portly and pink-cheeked, with the same tonsured hair as the other monks. With his round stomach and flowing, rust-coloured robes, the abbot reminded Emily of a squirrel. In other circumstances he probably would have been jolly, but now his shoulders sagged and his face was shadowed by despair.

Brother Lubek introduced the visitors. Among the Polish, they heard the words "England", "London" and "Queen Victoria". Then the young monk bowed and withdrew.

"I bid you welcome," Father Zachariasz said, spreading his hands wide. His English was excellent. "Sadly, a great pestilence has fallen upon our city. The number of sick people grows greater by the day, and no matter how many herbal potions we brew, it seems there is no cure."

"There is a cure," Filip said firmly. "But it is no herbal potion."

Father Zachariasz looked at Filip in surprise. He glanced at the young monk brewing herbs over the fire and then moved closer to the three visitors, lowering his voice. "Would you care to elaborate?"

Filip also lowered his voice. "Do you remember the bell that you sold to the Englishman, Sir Peter Walker, some weeks ago?"

"Ah, the Dhampir Bell." Father Zachariasz looked resigned. "Am I right in thinking that the bell has something to do with this plague? I never believed in the old stories about a disease which would be awoken by the chime of that bell. But now. . ." The abbot sighed. "Now I think I may have been a little hasty."

Emily saw Jack's exasperated frown. "If you knew about the old stories, why did you let the bell go?" he demanded.

Father Zachariasz tucked his hands into his threadbare sleeves. "I have asked myself the same question many times over the past few weeks, my son," he said gently. "And the answer is simple: money! Sir Peter offered a very large sum, and we at the house of St Wenceslaus are in desperate need of funds so that we can continue our charitable work across the city. At the time I saw no real harm in selling the bell, because I believed it to be nothing more than an interesting antique. But since then we have been visited by ever-increasing numbers of plague victims. I have been reading through the old manuscripts and I have come to realize that our only salvation may lie in the Dhampir Bell. But now it has been taken far beyond my reach to England."

"No, no," Filip said quickly. "The Dhampir Bell is here in Warsaw!"

Father Zachariasz looked amazed. "Here? But how. . . ?"

91

Filip quickly told the abbot how he had travelled to England to find Sir Peter. "I tried to stop him ringing the bell," he explained. "But I was too late. However, I believe there may still be a way to stop this plague."

"You mean by using the bell with the lost incantation," Father Zachariasz asked.

There was a stunned silence, and Emily exchanged a quick glance with Jack and Filip. "You *know* about that?" she asked.

The abbot smiled, his eyes almost disappearing into crinkled folds of skin. "I know about many things," he replied. "Although sometimes I wish I did not! Come with me. There is something I think you should see."

CHAPTER TWELVE

"This is the last patient, Doctor Cinska," Ben said. He had been working alongside Roman all morning, and felt as though he was almost back to his old self. Both Ben and Roman were surprised and pleased by the speed of Ben's recovery.

Now a thin, middle-aged woman with dark hair entered the consulting room. She was clearly suffering from the plague, and she was accompanied by her daughter, who looked similar in age to Ben himself.

"Ah, Madame Zagorska, and young Grazyna," Roman Cinska said, gesturing for the woman and her daughter to sit down. "I see you have already met my new assistant, Benedict Cole." Roman smiled encouragingly at the girl, Grazyna. "This is a good chance for you to practise your English, because young Benedict has travelled all the way from London to visit me here in Warsaw."

Grazyna smiled at Ben. "Pleased I am to be meeting

you," she said haltingly. Her voice was light and musical, and Ben realized that she would have been pretty if she hadn't been so pale and drawn.

"How is Madame Zagorska today?" Roman asked.

"My mother is so much worse, Doktor," Grazyna said tearfully.

"And you, Grazyna – how are you holding up?" Roman leaned forwards and held Grazyna's wrist lightly between thumb and forefinger, feeling for her pulse.

"I was well until yesterday. But last night and today I feel so tired – as if my bones are made of lead," Grazyna explained.

As he watched Roman take Grazyna's pulse, Ben noticed a deep scratch on the back of her left hand. It was about an inch long and crusted with dried blood.

"How did that happen?" Ben asked urgently, pointing to the scratch.

"Yesterday morning I am helping my mother to come downstairs," Grazyna replied. "But she is so weak that she lose her balance and almost fall. She grab hold of my hand to steady herself, and scratch me with her thumbnail."

Ben and Roman looked at Madame Zagorska's nails. They were long and sharp – and purple with the plague.

"The nails," Roman said softly. "This confirms what you and I have suspected, Ben. The disease can truly be spread through something as insignificant as a scratch!"

Grazyna bit her lip nervously. "Am I. . . Do I have the sickness too?"

Roman Cinska turned back to the girl and nodded gravely. "You do, Grazyna. But please do not be alarmed." The doctor adjusted his spectacles and picked up a glass phial full of serum. "I have developed a new medicine which will cure you, *and* your mother."

A relieved smile lit up Grazyna's face. "Oh, thank you, Doktor," she said. Then she added shyly, "And thank you too, Benedict."

"This is our scriptorium!" Father Zachariasz said, indicating the huge stone library with a sweeping gesture.

The abbot had led them along what seemed to Jack like miles of shadowy passageways, up staircases, and through draughty halls lined with ancient tapestries. Somewhere prayers were being chanted; Jack could hear the monks' voices rising and falling on the air.

Now the little group were standing in the middle of a huge chamber where stone pillars supported a high vaulted ceiling. A spiral staircase at one end of the room led upwards, finally disappearing into the shadows far above their heads. Shelves lined the walls, packed with rows of dusty leather-bound books and chronicles.

"And these are our scribes," Father Zachariasz said, indicating several monks perched on stools at sloping desks. Each of them was absorbed in their work, either illuminating manuscripts with feather quills dipped in vermilion ink, or making copies of Latin texts by candlelight. The abbot spoke softly to one of them and the scribe slid down from his stool and hurried away to climb the spiral staircase.

"Come and sit down," suggested Father Zachariasz, leading them to a desk in the corner of the room. "Brother Dominik will bring us the Tome. . ."

"The Tome?" Jack asked. He glanced hopefully at Emily.

She smiled. "A tome is a large and scholarly book," she explained. "Just like that one!" And she pointed to a monk who was making his way towards them with his arms clasped around a huge, dusty, leather-bound ledger. It was the size of a small suitcase, with elaborate bronze hinges that had turned green with age.

The monk, clearly Brother Dominik, lowered the ledger carefully on to the table in front of them, then bowed and withdrew.

Filip peered down at it, and his eyes widened in amazement. "The Dhampir Tome!" he gasped, glancing up at Father Zachariasz with an expression of disbelief. "The old legends say that it was destroyed in a fire. Yet it has survived here?"

"Hidden in our archives," Father Zachariasz confirmed with a nod. "Unused, unread – practically forgotten, until recently, when one of the Brothers of St Wenceslaus stumbled across it while cataloguing the volumes on the highest shelves of the library."

"What exactly is it?" Emily asked.

"Legend tells of the Dhampir Tome," Filip said, his voice still hushed with awe as he reached out to touch the cracked cover of the ledger with a trembling hand. "It is an ancient and very valuable book which has been handed down through generations of dhampirs, recording their struggles against lampirs. You remember, don't you, that a dhampir was a man – or woman – who had immunity to the lampir plague? Their line died out many years ago, but it is said that the information contained within this book is vital to anyone who wishes to defeat lampirism."

"May we open it?" Emily asked.

"Of course," Father Zachariasz said. "But be careful. Some of the pages are very fragile. Others are loose, as if someone wrote on spare scraps of paper and tucked them inside the book for safe-keeping. It is really a collection of writings, thoughts, drawings, folktales and general information about lampirs – I am sure some of it is exaggerated and wildly inaccurate."

Jack and Emily moved closer to Filip as he carefully opened the Dhampir Tome. The pages were thick, yellowing parchment, slightly rough at the edges as if each individual page had been trimmed by hand. There were sketches and maps and faded watercolour paintings of chapels with domed roofs. Many of the pages contained lines of close-knit script, so tiny as to be almost indecipherable.

A dry and dusty smell rose from the pages as Filip turned them. Jack raised his eyebrows; he'd thought reading Charles Dickens was hard work, this looked impossible!

"Most of it is in Polish," Emily said, frowning.

"Old Polish at that," Filip agreed. "Some of these writings at the beginning date from medieval times. I can barely understand them myself." He ran a finger across one of the pages and translated haltingly, "'Count Casimir Lampirska . . . feudal lord of Ornak, who was the father of lampirism. . . He seeketh eternal life by the use of dark magic. . . The women of Poland speaketh his name only in a whisper, for fear that his spirit may hear them and come to steal their babies.'"

Jack shuddered, watching as Filip turned another page.

"There is a paragraph here about dhampirs," Filip said, reading slowly. "'A dhampir is immune to attack from a lampir. Indeed a lampir is afraid of a dhampir, for the blood of a dhampir is like poison to the walking dead.'"

"Shame there ain't any dhampirs left alive then, ain't it?" Jack said flatly. "We could do with a drop or two of their blood!"

They dwelled on this in silence for a moment. Somewhere a scribe coughed, and a candle guttered and flared. Emily and Filip continued to consult the yellowed pages of the Dhampir Tome.

A few minutes later, Emily leaned forwards with a frown on her face. "*Cadaveris exsanguis* – that's Latin!" she exclaimed. "It means a dead person, without blood, no, *drained* of blood," she corrected herself.

"Indeed," Father Zachariasz agreed, nodding sagely. "There is much blood and death within these pages."

"There's more Latin here," Emily murmured, turning a page. She hesitated over the translation for a moment. "'A child –' no, that's *children* – 'A group of *children* were forced to flee from hordes of ravenous lampirs. They ran towards the mountains and were saved by dhampir riders, who shot the lampirs with flaming arrows'!"

"Flamin' arrows?" Jack grinned. "I like the sound o' them!"

"And here is something else," Filip put in, running his finger along a line of faded Polish writing. "'To have dhampir blood in one's veins is both a blessing and a curse.'"

Father Zachariasz nodded. "Yes, of course, it is a blessing to have the power to save lives, but a curse to know that there will always be some lives one cannot save."

Filip turned another page. On the other side of the scriptorium someone cleared their throat, and an elderly monk used a knife to sharpen his goose quill.

"Have you found anything about the lost incantation?" Jack asked after a while.

"Not yet." Filip turned several more pages. "There is so much information here to be sifted through and assessed. Some of it is probably exaggerated. Some of it may be no more than old wives' tales. There is much to translate and study and piece together. It could take several days for me to find the information we need – if it is here." He looked at Father Zachariasz. "May I have your permission to take the Tome away with me?"

The abbot looked doubtful. "This is a very old and valuable piece of Polish history which has been left in my keeping," he said. "I cannot allow it to be removed from the monastery."

"But it will be safe in my house," Filip assured him. "We have strong locks on all the doors. My brother is a doctor and he insists on good security so nobody can break in and steal his medicines."

"Even so, I would prefer the Tome to remain here in my care," Father Zachariasz insisted.

As the two men negotiated, Jack and Emily leaned over the Dhampir Tome once more.

"This is fascinating," Emily murmured. "There's so much information here. Look at this." She placed her finger under a line of Latin text. "This says that two hundred years ago the lampir plague struck a small village near the Carpathian Mountains in the south. Lampirs rose by the light of the moon and fed upon the blood of their relatives. The whole population was wiped out in less than a month!"

"Gruesome," said Jack. He glanced up to see that Filip seemed to have persuaded the abbot to lend him the Dhampir Tome. Filip was smiling and shaking Father Zachariasz warmly by the hand.

Emily drew Jack's attention back to the Tome. "Listen, Jack. This page lists all the things that give a person immunity to lampir attacks. 'Being infected with the sickness', well, we know all about that!"

She read silently for a moment, frowning over the words. "And it says here that if you take a length of hair from a dying plague victim, plait it, and wear it as a bracelet, it will protect you!"

Jack laughed. "Remember what Filip just said – some of the stuff in there is just old wives' tales," he reminded Emily. Then he peered over her shoulder, frowning. "Can you *really* understand all that Latin stuff?"

"Not every word," Emily admitted. "But enough to have a rough idea of what most of it means." She turned back to the Tome. "Now, this is interesting. . ." She grew suddenly still, her body tense.

"What is it?" Jack asked urgently. "What does it say?"

But there was no reply. Emily was translating the text, her lips moving silently as she ran her finger across the page. Finally she looked up at Jack, her eyes wide. "Jack, do you remember when the stagecoach was attacked, and that lampir backed away from you?"

Jack nodded. "How could I forget? We all thought I must have been infected."

"That's right! But I think it might have been something else that made the lampir back away," Emily breathed. She glanced back at the Tome, checking the text again. "It says here that if a person wears an item of jewellery, taken from one who died of lampir plague, then the wearer will be protected from all lampir attacks!"

Emily reached out and placed her fingertip on the heavy gold ring Jack wore on his middle finger: the ring that Molly had inherited from her grandmother; the ring that, on Molly's death, had come to Jack.

Jack looked down at the ring. "Molly's grandmother died of the lampir plague. . ." he said slowly.

"Exactly!" Emily agreed excitedly. "You weren't infected by a lampir, Jack. That wasn't why the lampir backed off. It was the ring! Molly's ring was protecting you!"

CHAPTER THIRTEEN

Ben looked down at the pale-faced young boy Roman was injecting with a dose of serum. The boy was called Albin Bubelski. Ben and Roman were in the small, cramped living room of the Bubelski family's home on Orezna Street. Standing at the grimy window, Ben could see the River Wisla through a gap in the buildings opposite. The river was frozen in parts and the long, arched bridge which crossed to the right bank was white with snow.

At noon, after administering the life-saving serum to Grazyna and her mother, Ben and the doctor had put on long coats and fur hats and set out from the Cinska townhouse, on foot, to do house calls. By mid-afternoon Ben had seen inside more than twenty Warsaw houses. Some were richly-furnished with high, airy ceilings, while others – like this one on Orezna Street – were cramped and stuffy, with threadbare rugs and shabby furniture.

Roman however, treated each patient as if he or she was the most important person he had seen that day. Observing him, Ben was beginning to think that he might rather be a doctor than a biologist when he was older.

Roman pressed a cotton pad to Albin's arm. The lad was the only one in the family to have the plague. His mother, father and little sister, Agata, had all miraculously escaped, and Roman wanted it to stay that way. He had already explained to the family that the plague could be transferred by the slightest scratch from one of Albin's fingernails, so now the little lad was wearing thick woollen gloves.

The doctor smiled and patted Albin on the head. Ben couldn't help thinking that the boy looked better already – a thought which warmed Ben's heart as he and Roman hurried home through the cold and snowy Warsaw streets.

That evening the friends shared the day's news over a delicious supper of spicy black-eyed pea soup and *kielbasa*, a chunky Polish smoked sausage. Ben was fascinated to hear about the Dhampir Tome, while Filip asked probing questions about the plague victims his brother had visited. It was past ten o'clock when they finally said goodnight to each other and went to bed.

The next morning, Jack was first down to breakfast. A

bright and cheery day had dawned. Outside, snow still lay on the ground but pale sunshine streamed into the dining room through white lace curtains. The housekeeper, Florentyna, was shuffling about, setting the table with silver lidded dishes and a large jug of something that looked like apple juice. She acknowledged Jack with a toothless grin and a few words in Polish.

There was no sign of Roman or Filip, but soon Emily and Ben breezed in. Florentyna ushered them all into chairs and indicated that they should help themselves to breakfast. Then she disappeared off to the kitchen.

No sooner had Florentyna exited than Roman entered the dining room. He sat down heavily without a word and stared morosely at the jug of apple juice. His clothes looked slightly crumpled, as if he'd slept in them, and his spectacles were covered in greasy smears.

Jack raised his eyebrows at Ben, who took the hint and said, "Good morning, Roman. Did you sleep well?"

"I barely slept at all!" Roman responded irritably. "Nightmares . . . nightmares . . . all through the darkest hours!"

"Perhaps you're working too hard," Emily suggested, pouring him a glass of juice. "You were still in the laboratory mixing serum when we went to bed last night."

Sighing, Roman took off his spectacles and began to polish them with his shirt-tail. "And still there is not enough medicine to treat every sick patient who comes to my door."

"I could help you again today," Ben offered.

"We all could," Emily said. "It's the least we can do. After all, you've been so kind in letting us stay here with—"

She was interrupted by the sound of the front door slamming, and footsteps hurrying along the hallway. Filip burst into the room, a long loaf of bread tucked under one arm and his long woollen scarf flapping wildly.

"I have just been to the bakery and heard the most extraordinary news!" he exclaimed. "Everyone is talking about it: a stagecoach was attacked last night, out on the main road to Thorn."

"Thorn?" Jack repeated. "Ain't that one of the towns we came through on our way here?"

Filip nodded. "The attackers felled a tree and placed it across the road to stop the coach," he went on breathlessly. "Then they murdered all the passengers."

"*Murdered!*" Emily breathed in horror. The friends all looked at each other in dismay.

At the far end of the table, Roman shrugged wearily. "It happens all the time," he said, jamming his spectacles on to the bridge of his bony nose. "Bandits are one of the hazards of modern travel."

"You think it was bandits, brother?" Filip put the loaf of bread down on the table heavily. "And yet, the woman

106

in the bakery told me that not a single thing was stolen from the victims, even though some were wearing valuable jewellery!"

Jack exchanged a worried glance with Ben and Emily. "Nothing was stolen?" he queried. "Even though everyone was *murdered*?"

"Murdered by being drained of blood!" Filip declared flatly. "And you know what that means: lampirs!"

"No!" Roman slammed the flat of his hand against the tabletop with such a loud bang that Jack nearly jumped out of his skin. He stared at the doctor, who was flushed with fury.

"This superstitious nonsense has to stop!" Roman shouted angrily at Filip. His spectacles glittered so that they couldn't see his eyes. "You talk so much of lampirs that I even dream of the wretched creatures!" Pushing back his chair, he stormed out of the dining room.

There was a small silence.

"Should someone go after him?" Emily asked uncertainly.

Filip shook his head looking puzzled. "Best to leave him alone," he sighed. "I don't know what is the matter with Roman this morning. Always we have these disagreements about the cause of the plague, but never before has my brother lost his temper in such a way."

"Maybe it's because he didn't sleep very well last night," Ben suggested.

Filip shrugged. "It is no excuse for rudeness in front of guests. I apologize, my friends."

"Please don't apologize," Emily said. "Roman has been working very hard. He's probably just tired and overwrought."

Jack stared at Emily and Ben incredulously. Why were they talking about manners and apologies when there was something far more important to be discussed? "Didn't you hear what Filip said?" he asked incredulously. "The attackers felled a tree! They placed it across the road to stop the coach!"

Emily, Ben and Filip looked at him blankly.

"Don't you see?" Jack asked. He pushed his chair back from the breakfast table and stood up. "The lampirs we've known so far have been a bit stupid. They've had no real intelligence, and no thought other than to blindly seek blood. But felling a tree takes planning and cunning. It means they've got together in some way. It means they're *organized*." Jack took a deep breath. "This ain't lampirs as we've known them – this is something new!"

CHAPTER FOURTEEN

"I fear you are right, my friend," Filip said, sounding worried. "We had better hope that I can find the lost incantation and stop them before they start planning bigger things. I shall go directly to my study and begin work on the Dhampir Tome."

"May I come with you, Filip?" Emily asked. "I could make notes and help with the Latin translations."

Jack glanced at Ben. They'd seen Emily at work on translations before, during their battle against the vampire-god Camazotz, and it was pretty dull for spectators.

Ben got the message. "Why don't we go and see if Roman needs a hand mixing some more serum?" he suggested.

"Good idea," Jack replied enthusiastically, and he and Ben hurried out of the room.

Down in the laboratory, Roman was working with a sample of infected blood, extracting a few drops from a test tube and adding them to a phial of serum to test its efficiency.

He glanced up as the boys came in. "If you have come down here to convince me that lampirs exist. . ." he began, glowering at them as the phial of serum fizzed between his fingers.

Jack shook his head. "Don't worry, Doc," he said. "We've come to help you mix up some more medicine, if you'd like us to."

Roman's face cleared. "Like you to?" he repeated. "I should be delighted! More hands will make light work, and there is much work to be done. Come, come. . ." He beckoned them to the workbench. "First I will teach you how to regulate the flame on the spirit lamp. . ."

Upstairs, in Filip's study, Emily frowned over a page in the Dhampir Tome. The little room was small but cheerful, with pale apricot walls, several pine bookcases, and a fire crackling merrily in the grate.

Filip was standing by the window with a book in his hands. "This is a study of the Old Polish language," he explained, licking his thumb and leafing through the pages. "It is written by a professor of Medieval Studies at Warsaw University. He was my tutor, and many years ago, when I was a student, he gave me a copy." Filip's eyes twinkled as he glanced over at Emily. "I am ashamed to say that this is the first time I have even opened it!"

Emily laughed. "Well, it's certainly going to come in

useful now," she said. "With your professor's book and this Latin dictionary, I think we should make good progress today."

An hour later, Filip gave a startled exclamation and looked up from his page of notes, his blue eyes wide. "Emily," he said. "I have made a discovery! I am reading here that twelve bells have been created over the years to defeat lampirism. All of them were forged by dhampirs, and all of them have been lost or destroyed over the centuries. Now, only one remains."

"Our Dhampir Bell," Emily breathed. She leaned forwards and peered at the page Filip was working on. There were densely-packed rows of faded brown script, and around the edge of the page it looked as though someone had been doodling: Polish script was interspersed with tiny religious symbols.

"If that section talks about the forging of the bells, does it mention the incantation?" Emily asked curiously.

"Oh, yes," Filip replied. "You see here. . . 'When the incantation is chanted and the bell chimes, then shall the dead be imprisoned within their graves.' I think the incantation is even written down here, but I cannot read it all."

"Why not?" Emily asked.

"You see these spots and smudges of brown ink?" Filip tilted the page so that she could see. "They have covered parts of the incantation, making it impossible to read the whole thing."

"I don't think that's brown ink, Filip," Emily said, biting her lip. "That's blood!"

Filip stared at the page again. "I believe you are right," he said eventually. "It chills my heart to think of how blood might have been spilled across the Dhampir Tome."

"Mine too," Emily said briskly. "But if we can't read those pages, we'll just have to hope that information about the incantation, or the incantation itself, has been written somewhere else in the book."

Filip took a deep breath. "Translating the whole Tome will take days!"

Emily shrugged. "I don't see that we have any other choice," she said.

For the rest of the day, Emily and Filip worked their way through the pages of the old ledger. Filip slowly translated while Emily took notes and looked up references for him in the various books and dictionaries piled on the desk. Ben brought them mugs of hot chocolate and sugary pastries in the afternoon. He, Jack and Roman had been out visiting patients, delivering Roman's serum all over the city.

On the way home, Ben told Emily, they had called in on Edwin Sherwood, and he had invited them all to join him for morning coffee at the hotel the next day.

Supper that evening was a subdued affair. Emily noticed that the boys didn't seem inclined to talk. Roman was tired, and Filip was obviously distracted by thoughts of his translations. He and Emily hurried back to his study the moment they had finished eating. But Emily's eyes ached from staring at old parchment for so many hours, and by the time the clock on the landing struck ten she was glad to escape to bed.

But in the middle of the night something woke her. She had been sleeping fitfully, dreaming about Old Polish, Latin and strange scribbled symbols. A man held his bleeding wrists towards her and said that he was a dhampir, and that his blood was poisonous to the walking dead. She woke to a cold, black, velvety darkness, her mouth dry and her heart pounding. A nightmare!

But then her ear caught the distant chime of a church bell. Was that what had woken her? She sat up and lit the candlestick on her bedside table. Then she heard it again – the sound of a man's laughter, followed by a muffled thump. The noises sounded as if they were coming from Roman's basement!

Emily quickly wrapped herself in her pale-blue dressing gown and crept downstairs. Her candle flame flickered on the walls and gleamed on the row of wooden chairs outside Roman's consulting room. Shielding the candle flame with one hand, Emily padded along the chilly hallway and down the steps towards the basement.

The door to the laboratory was half-open, and through the gap she could just make out the blue glow of the spirit lamp. Roman Cinska was hunched over his workbench with his back to the door, surrounded by blood samples and copper spoons and phials of powder in lurid greens and yellows. A balloon-shaped glass beaker of serum frothed and hissed on a stand over the spirit lamp.

Emily smiled to herself. The dedicated doctor was working late, mixing up more of his precious medicine. She decided not to disturb him, and quietly stole away.

But just as she began to make her way upstairs again, it occurred to Emily that perhaps Roman was working because he couldn't sleep. He'd been so tired and irritable that morning, complaining of nightmares. Perhaps she should go back down and offer to make him a cup of warm milk.

So Emily padded back down to the basement. But when she reached the laboratory she found that Roman had gone. Puzzled, she ventured further into the room, wondering if he had decided to lie down on the couch. But there was nobody there. Apart from a few flickering shadows cast by the blue flame of the spirit lamp, the room was completely empty!

Roman must have gone to bed, Emily decided. She blew out the spirit lamp and quietly closed the laboratory door behind her. But as she crept upstairs and climbed back into bed, a thought occurred to her: if Roman *had* gone to his room, how was it that they hadn't passed each other on the stairs?

CHAPTER FIFTEEN

"*Dziekuje*, Florentyna – thank you. That was a lovely breakfast," Emily said with a smile to the Cinskas' housekeeper, early the next morning. Working on the Dhampir Tome meant that Emily was learning basic Polish and she was pleased to see the old woman's face light up in a smile.

"Yes, those pancakes were great," Ben agreed with a grin, as Florentyna took his empty breakfast plate. "*Dziekuje!*" he told her.

"*To jest ni!*" Florentyna chuckled as she loaded a tray with the empty breakfast plates and shuffled out of the dining room. *You're welcome!*

"Very useful, Em," Jack said, sitting back in his chair. "What else have you learned?"

"*Jak sie pan miewa?*" responded Emily. "That means 'How are you?' But if you were a woman I should use the feminine form and say *pani* instead of *pan*!"

Filip smiled. "Polish, French, Latin and some Spanish,

too. Your sister is quite a linguist, Ben. She tells me that she also reads Mayan hieroglyphs."

Emily blushed. "Only because I had to decipher some old parchments last year when we were learning how to defeat Camazotz," she said modestly.

Just then Roman Cinska stumbled into the sunlit dining room and sat down at the breakfast table. He had overslept again, and looked even worse than he had the previous day. He was pale and dishevelled, his silk cravat was knotted untidily and his waistcoat was rumpled.

"*Jak sie pan miewa?*" Jack asked, with a good-natured grin.

But Roman didn't respond. He simply sat with his head in his hands, tufts of hair sticking out through his fingers.

"Brother, are you all right?" Filip asked, looking concerned. "Oversleeping two mornings in a row, this is not like you!"

"I apologize for my rudeness," Roman replied quietly. He gave a small groan and sat up straight, reaching for the teapot. "A glass of Florentyna's good strong brew should help me wake up."

Emily watched him pour the thick, treacly black liquid into a silver-handled glass, and was surprised to see the doctor's hand trembling. He spilled some tea on the pristine white tablecloth. Glancing at Roman's face, she saw that his eyes were red and bloodshot, as if he'd been rubbing them.

"You look very tired," she said sympathetically. "But I suppose that's not surprising, it must have been two in the morning by the time you went to bed."

Roman slugged back a mouthful of tea and shook his head. "No, no, Miss Emily. I was so exhausted last night that I went to bed before ten o'clock."

Emily frowned. "But I saw you in your laboratory in the early hours, mixing some serum."

"Impossible!" Roman replied.

"I *saw* you," Emily insisted. "A noise woke me and I came downstairs."

"My dear child, you must have been dreaming," Roman argued, giving her a tired half-smile. "Heaven knows, my own dreams are so vivid these days that I can quite understand someone thinking that they got out of bed when really they were in the midst of a dream." He shook his head morosely. "Or a *nightmare!*"

"I wasn't dreaming," Emily said firmly. She looked at Ben and Jack for support, but they both grinned at her as if they too thought she had dreamt the whole thing. Emily frowned in confusion. Was it possible that she *had* been dreaming? She thought about the possibility – and dismissed it. She was *certain* she'd seen Roman in his laboratory.

Just then, the front door bell rang. After a few moments, Florentyna shuffled back into the dining room with a young lad just behind her.

"Hello, Albin!" Ben exclaimed in delight. "You're looking much better today."

"Good morning," the lad said politely, bobbing his head.

As Florentyna left the room, Ben explained to Jack and Emily that Albin Bubelski was one of the patients he had helped Roman to treat the day before. Meanwhile, Albin was speaking quickly to Roman in Polish.

The expression on Roman's face changed from mild interest to alarm.

Jack turned to Filip. "What's Albin talking about?" he whispered urgently.

"The lad is saying that yesterday his mother, father and little sister did not have the sickness. Is that right, Ben – they were perfectly healthy?" Filip enquired.

Ben nodded.

"And yet overnight they became very sick. This morning Albin woke up to find them all dead."

"Then it can't have been lampir plague," Ben said quietly, staring at Albin, who was now gulping back tears. "It doesn't kill people overnight like that."

Filip shrugged. "And yet, he says they developed purple fingernails and milky eyeballs late last night."

"Sounds like lampir plague to me," Jack said.

By this time, Roman was on his feet. He put a comforting hand on Albin's shoulder and spoke gently to him in Polish. The lad nodded, and Roman put a plate of syrupy pancakes in front of him. Albin fell on the food as though he hadn't eaten for a week.

"Albin brings terrible news. I must go immediately to the house and see what can be done!" Roman said heavily.

"I'll come with you," Ben offered quickly.

"Yes, yes," Roman agreed. He glanced at Ben, obviously puzzled. "It's so strange, Benedict. The rest of the family showed no signs of illness yesterday."

"And even if they had," Ben put in, "it should have taken them twenty-one days to die, not less than twenty-one hours!"

Emily stood at the front door to watch her brother leave with Roman and young Albin. When she returned to the dining room, Filip was on his feet.

"This is most disturbing," Filip said, shaking his head. "If that family really have succumbed to lampir plague overnight then it can only mean one thing: the sickness is changing. It is somehow becoming even more deadly. The Dhampir Bell and the lost incantation are vital if we are to save Warsaw." He headed for the dining-room door. "I must get back to the Tome and find that chant!"

Emily started to go after him, but Jack seized her arm and held her back. "We're supposed to be meeting Edwin at the hotel this morning," he reminded her. "I can't go to the Syrena on my own. Edwin's not stupid. If you ain't with me, Em, he'll know that something's up."

Emily took a deep breath. "You're right. We'll go

together. The last thing I want is for poor Uncle Edwin to be dragged into our fight against lampirs! After all Sir Peter's disparaging remarks about his research, it's essential his work here in Warsaw goes well, otherwise the scientific community will never take him seriously!"

The only carriage for hire that Jack and Emily could find was an open landau – a two-wheeled two-seater that reminded Jack of the hansom cabs back in London. The top was open, folded back like a perambulator hood, and the driver – who spoke no English – mimed, apologetically, that it was broken.

"No problem, mate," Jack said cheerfully. "We'll just freeze!"

And freeze they did, because despite the pale winter sunshine the temperature in Warsaw was icy.

Emily perched on the seat opposite Jack, shivering. She was warmly wrapped in a fur collar, gloves, hat and scarf, but Jack noticed that the tip of her nose had turned scarlet even before they reached the end of the street. She hunched her shoulders up to her ears. "I wonder why there weren't any other carriages for hire?" she murmured.

"Dunno," said Jack, trying to stop his teeth from chattering.

But it wasn't long before they saw exactly why. . .

Every other carriage in the city had already been hired by someone else. As the landau clattered briskly over the straw-strewn cobbles, they saw coaches, Berlin carriages, and even rickety wagons being loaded with household goods. People were moving in and out of their houses with baskets and bundles which they piled high on whatever form of transport they'd managed to acquire. Some were even loading handcarts and barrows with their belongings.

Everywhere he looked, Jack saw grim-faced men battening wooden shutters over windows, and women with babies on their hips bolting doors and snapping padlocks.

"What are they doing?" Emily asked in a hushed tone.

"Everyone's leaving the city," Jack replied grimly. "They're scared of the plague . . . and they're running away."

CHAPTER SIXTEEN

The moment Albin let them into the house on Orezna Street, Ben could smell it: death. He knew by the cold, silent hush that there was no hope for anyone in that house. The look on Roman's face as he peered round the bedroom door told Ben the rest.

"Do not come through here, boys," the doctor said gently. "I will deal with this."

But Ben shook his head bravely. "I've seen death before, sir," he said calmly. "I watched my own father die last year. And I've seen horrors that you couldn't possibly imagine."

Roman looked at him for a long time. "You are a remarkable boy, Benedict," he said. "Come with me, then."

All three proceeded into the darkened bedroom. Albin's father and mother were lying side by side on the bed with little Agata between them. Their white faces were frozen in expressions of despair.

At the sight of them, Albin rushed to the bed and fell on his knees, burying his face in the blankets. Ben put a comforting arm around the lad's thin shoulders while Roman examined the Bubelskis.

The doctor pressed his thumb to Madame Bubelski's eyelids and inspected her eyes. "Some cloudiness is a natural event after death," he said. "But this mist has completely covered the iris – the coloured part of the eye. Yesterday I noticed that this woman had brown eyes, but today there is no colour to be seen. This is very common in plague sufferers. I saw the same milky film in your eyes when you had the plague, Benedict."

Roman sighed and covered the family with a sheet. "There is no doubt in my mind – the family did indeed die of the plague. But the question is, why was it so rapidly fatal? I have never seen a case where the victim died in anything less than twenty-one days—"

He was interrupted by a frantic rapping on the door. "Doktor! Doktor!"

Ben and Roman hurried outside to find a woman on the front doorstep. It was Madame Zagorska, Grazyna's mother. She looked frantic with worry, and Ben felt his heart begin to pound. Had something happened to Grazyna?

He waited, feeling slightly sick, as Roman questioned Madame Zagorska. "It is her husband and mother," the doctor explained after a moment. "They too have been struck down overnight, as have many of their neighbours." He ran his hand through his hair, visibly distressed. "Benedict, this is an extremely aggressive form of the plague. I don't know if my serum can cure it!"

Madame Zagorska spoke again and Roman nodded, calming her with a quiet word.

Then he turned to Ben, "It is customary in Poland – as I expect it is in England – for the dead to lie in state. The coffins are left open for some days here, usually in the front parlour. But I shall insist that these plague victims are buried *immediately*, in order to cut down on the chances of others being infected."

"Buried?" asked Ben. He swallowed hard. "Er, Roman. There's something you should know. The only way to prevent more deaths is to burn the bodies."

"Burn them?" Roman frowned. "I do not think that will be necessary."

"It's vital that once these people are dead, they *stay* dead," Ben pointed out. "And burning the bodies is the only way to be sure!"

He knew immediately that he had said too much. Roman turned bright red, and a muscle in his jaw twitched.

"You have been listening to my foolish brother and his talk of lampirs," the doctor said tightly. "I am only thankful that poor Madame Zagorska cannot understand English. It would distress her beyond measure to hear you talk of burning her family in case the dead should wake! Now –" he twitched his waistcoat straight – "I shall send for the undertaker, and then we shall return to the house and begin work on a new, stronger serum. And I will tolerate no more talk of lampirs. Do I make myself clear?"

"Crystal," said Ben flatly.

That evening a subdued Jack, Ben and Emily ate supper alone. Earlier, Roman had carried a plate of bread, sausage and cheese up to his bedroom, saying that he was so exhausted he planned to eat alone and then go to bed early. Filip was still in his study, working on the Dhampir Tome.

Emily had taken Filip a glass of tea and she reported that he might be making some progress. "He didn't say much," she admitted, when the others asked her to elaborate. "And I didn't like to question him in case I broke his concentration."

Florentyna had left a tureen of *barszcz*, a hearty beef soup, in the oven. The three friends carried this up to the dining room. They ate slowly, dipping in chunks of homemade brown bread smeared with sour cream, as they discussed the events of the day.

"I saw folk preparing to leave, too," Ben said with a nod. He frowned and licked sour cream off his thumb. "How was Uncle Edwin? Does he know what's happening?"

Jack shook his head. "The symposium is in a world all

of its own. The delegates' heads are so full of ancient cultures that they ain't noticed what's going on in the here and now!"

"Poor Uncle Edwin seems to spend most of his time racing from the hotel conference suite on the ground floor, to the organizers' office upstairs, and back again," Emily put in. "And he's constantly shuffling pieces of paper – tickets for this lecture or that talk, speech notes, invitations and requests from other archaeologists. . . He's drowning in paper!"

Just then Filip came into the dining room. There were inkstains on his fingers and his blond hair was sticking up even more wildly than usual.

"Drowning in paper?" Filip said, helping himself to a chunk of bread and dipping it into the soup tureen. "I know exactly how Edwin is feeling! But, my friends, I have good news at last!"

"The incantation?" Emily asked eagerly. "You've found it?"

Filip swallowed his bread with a smile. "Part of it, but not all. Emily, you remember those lines of Polish script interspersed with religious symbols – what did you call them, *doodles*?"

"Yes. It looked as though someone had decorated the edge of the page," Emily replied.

"Indeed. Well, I have discovered that these doodles are an inscription which forms part of the incantation itself!" Filip explained, his eyes sparkling.

Jack and Ben looked at each other. "That's great!" Jack exclaimed. "So can we go out and start ringing the Dhampir Bell?"

"Alas, no," Filip sighed. He took a bowl and ladled soup into it. "Emily may have told you that some of the pages are smeared with blood. Unfortunately, those smears obscure some of the words, so there are several gaps in the incantation. And of course we need all of it for the ritual to be effective."

"Oh," Jack said, looking slightly crestfallen.

"Do not be downcast," Filip said cheerfully. "We are making progress! All we need to do now is find another reference to the incantation, and fill in the gaps!"

CHAPTER SEVENTEEN

Silvery moonlight slanted across Emily's room. A floorboard creaked out on the landing and Emily held her breath. Outside in the street a wagon rolled past, the iron-rimmed wheels ringing on the cobbles. Somewhere a dog barked.

And inside the house, another floorboard creaked.

Heart pounding, Emily threw back the covers and hurried to press her ear to her bedroom door. She had stayed awake for hours, lying in bed, fully-clothed, waiting for this to happen. But now that the moment was here, she wasn't sure what to do. Should she wake Ben and Jack?

But, no, she'd seen their faces when Roman had insisted she'd been dreaming. They hadn't believed her. No one had! But Roman *had* been in his laboratory in the middle of the night. So why had he denied it? It didn't make sense – unless there was something sinister going on. Emily was determined to find out.

Carefully, she eased open her bedroom door and felt her way along the hall in the darkness. There was a flickering light down in the hallway. But even as she watched, the glow disappeared as if whoever was holding the candle had disappeared down the steps to the basement. She was certain it was Roman!

Keeping one hand on the wall to steady herself, Emily crept downstairs after him. The laboratory door was ajar. Peeping through the gap, Emily could see Roman bending over the workbench. He lit the spirit lamp and turned the flame up high. Shadows reared and leaped on the walls, dancing with the blue flame.

Then Roman set a balloon-shaped glass beaker of serum over the spirit lamp to heat. Muttering to himself in Polish, he carefully measured out a spoonful of dark-coloured crystals which he began to grind with the mortar and pestle. Emily wondered what the dark crystals were. They certainly were not Allium Sativum, which she knew to be bright yellow. Clearly the doctor was concocting a completely new kind of serum.

Emily watched as the doctor added the crushed crystals to the mixture, making the strange new serum fizz violently into a thousand plum-coloured bubbles. Roman chuckled to himself as he swirled the glass beaker to mix the contents. When the new serum had settled and turned clear, he poured it into a large, flask-like container and pressed a chunky cork into the neck.

Then he snatched up his coat from the back of a chair and shrugged it on.

Emily suddenly realized that Roman was about to leave the laboratory, and she was right in his pathway!

Frantically she looked round for a place to hide. But there was nowhere. Horrified at the thought of being caught, she darted back up the steps and along the hallway. The only place to hide was the consulting room. She slipped in and crouched behind the door, praying that Roman would not stop to collect anything from in there. She could hear his heavy tread on the basement steps. He was drawing closer! In fact, he was coming into the consulting room. . .

Emily squeezed herself tightly into the space between the door and the wall, glad that she was wearing a dark dress which would help her blend into the shadows. She held her breath and watched as Roman advanced into the room, holding his candle high. The light flickered over the glass cabinets full of pill pots and the varnished wooden desk. Shadows shimmered and shifted. Roman opened a small cupboard and rooted around, obviously looking for something. Glass syringes clattered to the floor. Eventually, the doctor gave a grunt of satisfaction and slipped something into his coat pocket. Then he was gone, the front door snapping shut behind him.

Emily gave a sigh of relief and stood up. She was determined to follow Roman Cinska and find out where he was going with this strange new serum. Briefly, she considered waking Jack and Ben, but she quickly decided that there wasn't time. She didn't want to risk losing track of Roman.

Grabbing her coat from the hat-stand in the hall, Emily let herself out of the house. She glanced left and right, and for a moment thought that she was too late – Roman had disappeared. But then she saw him, right at the far end of the deserted street, walking quickly with a purposeful stride.

She hurried after him. There was a hush in the air and the temperature had dropped well below freezing. Emily could feel her lungs chilling as she breathed in the icy air. Moonlight glittered on the frosty cobbles and she knew she'd have to be careful not to slip.

Roman headed north through the city, along narrow streets and past dark houses and churches. He moved fast, and Emily had trouble keeping up. But then he stopped suddenly and she had to shrink into the shadows beneath an arched bridge. Her heart was hammering so loudly she was sure Roman would be able to hear it.

She watched as he knocked on the door of a house at the end of a row of well-kept townhouses. After a moment the door opened and a man in a dressing gown and a woolly night-cap peered out. He obviously recognized Roman, because he smiled and made a gesture as if to welcome the doctor into his home.

Roman shook his head and spoke in a low voice. The

man in the night-cap called over his shoulder and soon a woman and a young man appeared, also in dressing gowns. The family waited patiently as Roman reached into his coat pocket and produced the corked flask and a handful of tiny glass pots. He gave a little pot to each person, and then carefully measured out three doses of the new serum.

"*Dziekuje!*" said the man in the night-cap, and he swallowed his dose. His wife and son did the same, then they all bid farewell to the doctor and disappeared back inside the house.

This happened at four or five more homes. Roman Cinska dispensed the new serum to several families, as Emily watched from the shadows, blowing on her hands to keep them warm. She guessed that Roman must have developed a medicine which would protect healthy people from catching the plague. But she couldn't help wondering, if that was the case, why he hadn't celebrated this wonderful achievement with herself, Ben, Jack and Filip, or why he'd denied that he'd been working through the night to create it. It didn't make sense. In fact, the more Emily thought about it, the more convinced she became that something was very wrong.

She hurried on through the night, following Roman from street to street. Suddenly, she heard raised voices up ahead and saw five or six men spilling out of a tavern, arguing drunkenly. One of them roughly shoved his neighbour in the chest, and at that, another threw a punch.

Emily glanced at Roman, who was drawing very close to the rowdy group, and saw that he had paused in a patch of silvery moonlight, clearly nervous about getting drawn into a drunken brawl. For a moment, he simply stood there, then, as the men staggered down the street towards him, Roman Cinska suddenly vanished into thin air!

CHAPTER EIGHTEEN

Still arguing, the men turned off down a side street, and abruptly Emily was alone. Her heart pounding, she stared at the spot where she had last seen Roman. He had simply vanished, melted into the shadows – like a lampir! Her stomach clenched and she felt sick. Where was he now?

And then she saw a dark shadow, like a pool of tar, rippling swiftly across the snowy cobbles. The shadow, Emily realized, was heading in the same direction that Roman had been taking, and she knew at once that it was the doctor in shadow-form. She took a deep breath and hurried after him.

As she walked, Emily's mind raced. She was fairly certain that Roman *couldn't* be a lampir. After all, lampirs couldn't walk around in daylight, and she'd clearly seen Roman sitting in a pool of winter sunshine at the breakfast table only this morning. Besides, he'd shown no signs of infection. And yet, here he was, stalking the streets after dark – as a shadow.

Up ahead, Roman's shadow turned right and crossed a moonlit market square, then rippled up a short flight of stone steps to a higher street on another level. Carefully keeping her eyes on the shadow, Emily followed at a safe distance, turning over the possibilities in her mind.

She remembered the explosion in the laboratory on their first day in Warsaw. Shards of glass had scratched Roman's arm. Was it possible that somehow the serum had entered his bloodstream? The serum had cured Ben of lampir plague, but Roman hadn't been ill, so what if the mixture had had a different effect on him? What if the precious serum that cured *infected* blood had a rather more sinister effect on the healthy blood of an uninfected person? Roman had seemed entirely unaffected by the serum at the time, but now Emily began to think that it had actually affected him in the worst way possible, turning him into a strange hybrid: half-human, but also *half-lampir*!

Suddenly, she realized that Roman had stopped, and she quickly drew back into a doorway. They had arrived at an enormous archway in a high stone wall. Beyond it, Emily could see snow-covered tombstones. Some lay flat on the ground while others stood upright, silhouetted against the night sky.

It was a cemetery.

But this was not a well-ordered, English cemetery, like those Emily had seen in London. This Warsaw necropolis was something altogether larger and wilder. Huge tombs that looked like small houses were crammed together in zigzag rows, some so close together that there was barely space for a blade of grass in between. Towering trees trailed skeletal branches along the ground, like black weeping willows. And the moon shone down, highlighting the scene in spectral silver.

Roman's shadow rippled onwards through the stone archway, and Emily's skin turned cold as she realized they were going in. *Being alone, in a cemetery, with a half-lampir at dead of night is a bad idea*, she thought. But she wasn't about to turn back; she was determined to see what Roman was up to.

Keeping well back, Emily followed the doctor's shadow under low-hanging branches, past tumbledown crosses, and around the outstretched arms of marble angels. Then abruptly, she stopped, and ducked behind a tombstone.

They had come to a clearing. And Roman was in human-form once more. Holding her breath, Emily peered out just in time to see the doctor step up on to a small marble platform that was part of a broken tombstone. He flung his arms wide, and tipped his head back to stare up at the night sky. Silvery moonlight shone down upon him, clearly illuminating his features, and for a moment Emily didn't recognize the evil, twisted face as Roman's.

Suddenly, he started to speak in Polish. Emily

struggled to pick out a word or two that she understood, but there weren't any.

"Podniescie sie z grobow i walczcie. . ." he chanted.

An arctic wind whipped across the necropolis, dashing loose snow into Emily's eyes and stinging her cheeks. The trees shivered in the breeze as if they were cold, and the ground seemed to heave beneath Emily's feet. She heard a low moaning sound behind her, and twisted round in time to see hundreds of black shadows gliding across the snow towards her. Lampirs!

Even as Emily took this in, the earth cracked and the tombs began to shake. Monuments toppled, the graves of the dead were torn open, and hideous figures ripped themselves from the earth, baying for blood.

Emily stared in horror as legions of lampirs rose from the snowy ground and arranged themselves in rows around Roman.

"Bacznosc. . .!" Roman commanded. And the lampirs snapped to attention. They held themselves stiffly with their shoulders back and jaws firm, like soldiers at a passing-out parade. There were three platoons, one on either side of Roman and one in front. He was obviously their General, for he snapped a series of orders and two files of lampirs obediently peeled off from the central section and began to march away. As they moved, they seized makeshift weapons: wooden staves, broken bits of stone, and sharp metal railings. Some of them used their superhuman strength to snap

the limbs from marble angels, holding them like clubs.

Meanwhile, Roman was still giving orders. The wind whipped his voice away so that Emily was forced to creep closer in order to hear what he was saying. She crouched behind a gravestone and listened. Most of what Roman said made no sense to her, but thanks to her studies with Filip she could grasp the occasional word. *Bramy*, that meant "gates", Emily knew. And *drogi* were "roads" – she'd seen that word on street signs. She frowned, her mind racing as she listened to Roman Cinska's commands. *Most*, she thought that meant "bridge", but she couldn't piece the words together to work out what Roman was saying.

Most of the remaining lampirs armed themselves and marched away like a ragged, skeletal army. She could hear their rasping breath, and the low, guttural death rattle that chilled her blood.

And then it hit her. Roman was telling the lampirs to surround the city. He wanted them to close the city gates, block the roads, shut off access to the bridge. His army was besieging Warsaw. There would be no escape, and soon every healthy citizen would succumb to this new, virulent form of lampir plague!

Emily bit her lip so hard she tasted blood. Jack had been right – these lampirs were organizing themselves, and now she knew why. It was because they had a new and powerful half-lampir to lead them: Roman Cinska. She squeezed her eyes shut for a moment and leaned her head back against the gravestone behind her. What could she do to stop him?

But then Roman uttered some more words that Emily recognized: words that chilled her to the bone.

"Filip Cinska . . . Jack Harkett . . . Benedict . . . Emily Cole. . . *Zabijcie ich i wszystkichi przyniescie mi dzwonek!*"

Emily knew that *dzwonek* meant "bell", she'd seen it written time and time again in the Dhampir Tome. But what was Roman saying? Why had he named them all, and mentioned the bell?

Emily watched as the last lampirs – about twenty in all – responded to Roman's curt commands and began arming themselves. Clutching sticks and broken railings in their claw-like hands, they didn't look as if they were intent on a mission of peace. And all at once, Emily understood. Roman had ordered the lampirs to find Filip, Jack, Ben and herself, and seize the Dhampir Bell!

Emily whirled around, ready to head back to the house and warn her brother and her friends, but as she did so, the heel of her boot turned a loose stone. *Crack!* – the sound ricocheted across the cemetery like a gunshot.

Her heart thundering, Emily threw herself face first into the snow. But it was too late. The lampirs had heard her, and as she lifted her head to peer around the edge of a nearby gravestone, she saw that Roman Cinska was staring directly at her hiding place.

CHAPTER NINETEEN

Emily pressed herself flat to the frozen ground again. Had Roman seen her? She could hear him rasping a set of orders.

She raised her head again, just enough to see what was happening. To her horror, about twenty lampirs were lumbering towards her hiding place, weapons raised. Their milky-white eyeballs rolled as they scanned left and right, looking for her. Then they began to spread out, fanning wide across the dark cemetery.

Emily scrambled to her feet and darted away, stooping low to keep her head below the level of the tombstones. Angels and crosses flashed past. Diving across an area of open ground, she threw herself headlong behind a low, flat tomb. She lay motionless in the shadows, holding her breath and praying that she hadn't been seen.

Behind her, the lampirs grunted and growled. Their heavy footsteps shook the frozen earth; some of them were coming closer. Carefully lifting her head, Emily peered over the top of the low tomb. She could see three lampirs. One was an old woman with wispy white hair. Her skeletal finger-bones were bursting through the rotten flesh of her hands. The other two were young men who appeared to have died quite recently, judging by their smooth skin and fresh clothes. One looked particularly smart in a starched white shirt with a high collar and a silky cravat.

Emily's heart pounded as the three lampirs lurched closer. They were only yards away now. She knew that they would be on top of her in just a few short moments. . .

Emily realized she couldn't stay where she was. She had to risk moving. Holding her breath, she eased herself up on to hands and knees and crawled quietly away. Through the drooping branches of a nearby tree, she could see the stone archway which marked the entrance to the cemetery. That would be her first goal – just to get that far.

Taking a deep breath, Emily lunged for the nearest tree, and flattened herself tight against the trunk. She was in shadow, but all around her moonlight dappled the earth. She prayed that a ragged cloud would pass in front of the moon, and give her temporary cover so that she could run with less likelihood of being seen.

Meanwhile, the lampirs were still drawing closer. They were speaking in a garbled tongue, a strange guttural sound that was only half-human. Peering out

141

from behind the tree, she watched as the old woman grunted something to the two young men. They were clearly communicating. This was another sign that these lampirs had developed beyond the zombie-like beings the friends had battled in London. Emily squeezed her eyes tightly shut, wishing that she had woken Ben and Jack before setting off in pursuit of the doctor.

But there was no time for regrets now. A quick glance showed Emily that the two young men had veered off away from her tree. She could see their hunched figures loping between statues and shrines. The old woman was closer, but she had turned her back and was scanning the graveyard.

Emily left the shelter of the tree and began to run towards the stone archway, dodging tumbledown gravestones and angels. Twigs snatched at her hair. Cold air froze her lungs and she was hampered by her wet skirts and petticoats, but the stone archway was getting closer. Somewhere a wolf howled, and behind her, the old lampir-woman suddenly let out a screech which seemed to rip the night apart. Others joined in, baying for blood. One quick glance over her shoulder was enough for Emily to realize that they had seen her!

She snatched up her petticoats and ran faster than she had ever run before. Blood pounded in her ears. Tombs flashed past in a blur. Emily stumbled and glanced back over her shoulder again – just in time to see four or five lampirs slip into shadow-form. They could travel faster as shadows and now they came rushing across the ground, rippling over the gravestones, and moving so quickly that Emily knew she couldn't outrun them. But still, she pushed herself on, faster and faster, gasping for breath, until her legs and lungs ached with the effort of running.

All at once, a black shadow rippled beneath her feet. She dodged sideways as the lampir reared up in human-form and swiped at her face with a clawed hand. It was a man, dead so long that his flesh was dry and brown like leather. Tendons and muscles were horribly visible, little more than strings to work his jaws and hold his bones together. With a horrified scream, Emily ducked and plunged on beneath his outstretched arms.

And then he was behind her. Emily felt a tug at her hair, as if the creature had tried to catch hold of her but missed. His howl of frustration rang in her ears, but she kept running. Her lungs burning with the effort, Emily bolted the last few yards to the gate. Shadows swirled around her and some of the lampirs started to rematerialize into human-form. Skeletal fingers reached for her coat, her hair, her arms. . . And then at last she was through the stone archway and out on to the open road. She almost fell under the wheels of a fast-moving landau carriage. The driver swore in Polish and hauled on the reins, and Emily just had time to make out a face that she recognized. It was their coach driver from yesterday: the one who'd taken Emily and Jack to the Hotel Syrena.

"Please. . ." Emily gasped, wracking her brains for the word in Polish. "*Prosz*, help me!" She glanced over her shoulder and saw dozens of lampirs approaching at a run. They were all in human-form now, fangs glittering in the silver moonlight.

The landau driver took one look at them all and yelled, "*Lampir!*" Bunching the reins in one powerful hand, he seized a huge handful of Emily's coat with the other and hauled her up on to the bench behind him. Weak with relief, Emily clung to the seat, as the driver whipped up his horse.

The closest lampir snarled and threw itself at the carriage. Its bony fingers caught the edge of the driver's seat, but the driver simply brought his whip down on them hard. There was a terrible screeching sound and the lampir fell backwards. It hit the road with a dull thud and disappeared, crushed beneath the landau's iron-rimmed wheels.

All that was left was the lampir's hand, twitching as it tried to keep a grip on the seat. With a shudder of revulsion, Emily leaned across the driver and plucked the hand off the seat. She threw it away as hard as she could, and heard it smash against the cemetery wall.

The landau raced on into the city.

* * *

"Wake up!"

Ben woke with a start to find Emily bent over him, her face eerily lit by the oil lamp in her hand. She was shaking him hard by the shoulder.

"Wake up, Ben," she hissed again.

He sat up and she darted across the room to shake Jack awake too. It was then that he noticed she was wearing her outdoor coat.

"*Wha –?*" Jack sat bolt upright in his bed, nearly knocking the oil lamp out of Emily's hand. "What's going on?" He rubbed his eyes. "Why are you dressed, Em? You're all wet! Have you been outside?"

Emily nodded. "I stayed awake and listened for Roman. He went down to his laboratory and made a batch of some new sort of serum. And then he went out of the house. I followed him. He stopped at different households, giving people doses of his new medicine, until finally he got all the way to a cemetery on the other side of the city."

Jack stared. "You followed him on your own? That was brave. . ."

"Why didn't you wake us up?" Ben demanded.

"I'm waking you up now," Emily replied tightly. "Come on, get dressed. We haven't got much time!" She was seizing handfuls of clothing from a chair by the window and flinging them at Ben and Jack.

Ben caught his breeches and shirt in one hand. "You should have taken us with you," he said crossly. "Why didn't you wake us?"

Emily sighed. "Because you didn't believe me yesterday, when I said Roman had been up in the night!" she told him.

Ben felt himself go red. "I'm sorry," he said, pulling his breeches on and buttoning his braces. "We should have listened. But I still don't think you should have gone out on your own in the dead of night."

Emily rolled her eyes to the ceiling. "If I hadn't, we'd all be fast asleep in bed. And nobody would know that an army of lampirs is heading this way!"

"*WHAT?*" Ben and Jack both cried at once.

"That's what I've been *trying* to tell you! Honestly, I am capable of doing things without you, you know!" Emily replied, sounding exasperated.

She turned her back as Jack began to tug off his pyjama top. "Do you remember when the glass beaker exploded in the laboratory?" she asked. "Roman got scratched by flying glass and I think some of the serum got into his body. Well, I think it's affected him in a strange way. Now he's only half-human, and—"

"Hang on, Em," Ben interrupted, shrugging his jacket on. "If the doctor's only *half*-human, what's his other half?"

"Lampir," Emily said flatly. "I saw him use shadow-form to slip through the streets tonight. And when he got to the cemetery he commanded hundreds of lampirs. Roman's built himself an army. He's sent some of the lampirs to block every route out of the city. The rest of them are coming here. They want the Dhampir Bell."

Jack was dressed and ready. "I'll wake Filip," he said. "We have to get the bell out of here before they come." He hesitated, one hand on the door. "But where are we going to go? And how are we going to get there?"

"The landau driver is waiting out in the street," Emily replied. "And I think the safest place to go will be the Hotel Syrena and Uncle Edwin."

"Right!" Jack was gone, taking the stairs two at a time to Filip's room at the top of the house.

"Well done, Em," Ben said, looking at his sister admiringly. She seemed to have thought of everything. "How long have we got before the lampirs get here?"

"As long as it takes them to run across the city." She shrugged. "Ten minutes? Maybe less. Why?"

"We need to have a closer look at this new serum Roman's made."

"But there's no time!" Emily exclaimed.

"There is if we stop wasting it standing here!" Ben said, making for the door. "I'm going down to the laboratory. We have to know what it is Roman has created."

Ben raced down to the basement with Emily close behind him. He went straight to the workbench. A glass beaker with about half an inch of a clear fluid in it was poised over the spirit lamp.

"Is this it?" Ben asked. And when Emily nodded, he frowned. "But it looks just like the serum Roman used to cure me."

Emily shook her head. "No, this one's different, Ben. The other mixture turned bright green when Roman added the Allium Sativum. And it turned infected blood into healthy blood." She pointed to the clear liquid in the beaker. "This serum turned the colour of plums before it eventually settled."

"Plums?" Ben frowned. "Plums are purple."

"Exactly. And purple is a colour we've come to associate with lampirs – their fingernails and their blood are both purple," Emily pointed out. She bit her lip. "Ben, I think Roman has been making a serum which actually makes people into lampirs."

They both stared at each other in dismay.

Suddenly a floorboard creaked on the stairs outside, and Emily whispered, "Someone's coming!"

"There you are!" Jack said, stepping into the laboratory. "Filip's got the bell and I've got the Dhampir Tome. Now, let's go!" But to his astonishment, his friends both shook their heads.

"We have to test this serum," Ben said urgently. He poured a measure of clear liquid into a glass phial.

Emily nodded as she took a needle from the workbench and bravely pricked her own finger. "It's important that we know what we're dealing with, Jack."

"Have you two gone stark, raving mad?" Jack cried, hitching the oil-cloth-wrapped book higher on his hip.

"There's no time for experiments! A lampir army is coming this way!"

Filip had obviously heard their voices. He had the big blue hat-box containing the Dhampir Bell clutched in his arms as he came hurrying into the basement. He was just in time to see Emily add a gleaming droplet of her own healthy blood to the serum in the phial.

It sank to the bottom, and for a moment nothing happened. Jack let out the breath he found he'd been holding. Then, without warning, the serum began to fizz violently. A thousand purple bubbles rose all the way to the neck of the phial. A terrible stench rose in the air, and clouds of smoky, sulphurous vapour filled the room. Everyone coughed as the gas tore at their noses and throats. Then, abruptly, the vapour cleared, the serum settled, and there was the droplet of Emily's blood. Except that it wasn't Emily's red, healthy blood any more. Now, floating in the serum, was a droplet of shimmering, glistening purple blood. And all around it, the serum was tinted purple too.

There was silence as everyone took in the significance of the experiment.

"This potion makes healthy blood into infected blood," Filip said hoarsely. "Obviously it is a lampir-creating serum. And my brother made it!" He groaned. "Oh, Roman. What have you done?"

"No wonder there's a bloomin' epidemic in the city!" Jack exclaimed. "The good doctor's been goin' round infecting folk with his nice new medicine! We have to stop him."

"There's no time to think about that now," Emily said briskly. "We have to get the Bell and the Tome to a safe place before the lampirs get here. After that, we can think about how to stop Roman."

Ben nodded. "Em's right. Those lampirs will be here any minute now!" he said, glancing at the laboratory door. "Let's go."

The friends made their way quickly upstairs and along the hallway. Moonlight played across the floor in silvery stripes, streaming in through the glass panels in the front door.

Filip was in front of the others. Suddenly he stopped. "Look!" he said in a strange voice.

"What?" Jack asked, peering over Filip's shoulder. And then he saw it: there, silhouetted in black against the door's glass panels, was a sight which made his blood run cold. "A lampir!" Jack breathed in horror.

And, as he stared, it was joined by another. And another.

CHAPTER TWENTY

"The landau driver!" Emily gasped, and she made a dash for the front door.

But Jack held her back.

"I think the driver's dead, Em," Ben said flatly.

Jack turned to Filip. "What do we do now?" he asked.

"We go out the back way," Filip replied. "Through the kitchen. Run!"

Burdened by the heavy Dhampir Tome, Jack dashed back along the hallway behind Ben and Emily. He heard a muttered oath from Filip, and knew that the lampirs were probably dissolving into shadow-form, ready to slip under the door. Jack felt a shiver of fear. Lampirs were no ordinary vampires. It was no good forbidding them entry to a house. They just came in anyway, oozing across the threshold like pools of black blood, before rematerializing in human-form – *inside* the house!

Jack heard a hissing sound behind him, and knew it was an intake of breath passing between sharp fangs.

The lampirs were in the house. "Hurry!" he whispered to Ben and Emily.

Emily was first through the kitchen door. Ben tumbled after her, then Jack, and finally Filip. They found themselves in a small square room with Florentyna's black cooking-range in one corner.

"The back door!" exclaimed Filip. "The key is hanging on the hook – there!"

Ben seized the key, thrust it into the lock, turned it and wrenched on the door handle. But the solid oak door didn't budge. "It's stuck!" Ben yelped.

Behind them, a lumbering tread echoed down the hallway, followed by a series of guttural grunts. The lampirs were coming.

"The bolts!" Filip gasped. "I forgot. There are bolts at the top and bottom of the door."

Shoving the blue hat-box at Emily, Filip reached up high and shot the top bolt back, while Ben did the one at the foot of the door. Then, mercifully, the door swung open and a rush of icy air met them as they dashed outside into a small, paved yard, surrounded by ten-foot high walls.

Jack saw immediately that there was nowhere to run – no gate, no door, no exit at all. "We're trapped!" he cried, spinning round as he scanned the walls.

"Not trapped," Filip said firmly. He slammed the back door shut and locked it with the key. Then he stripped off his jacket and stuffed it into the gap beneath the door. "Help me," he said to Ben. "We must buy ourselves a little time."

"Good idea!" Ben replied. He took out his white cotton handkerchief and stuffed it in the keyhole. "The shadows can't come through if there isn't a gap, or any glass!"

When they had filled all the gaps in the door with cloth, Filip ran over to a little wooden outhouse. He gestured for Emily to come closer. "I will hold the bell while you climb up," he told her. "See, there is a little foothold there, on the window ledge. You go on to the roof, and then over the wall. The drop the other side is not so bad. The lane there is on a higher level. Quickly, now. . ."

With a determined look on her face, Emily tucked up her skirts and petticoats, and began to climb. She was up on the roof, spraying feathery snow down on them, before Jack even had time to say, "Be careful!"

The kitchen door handle twisted and rattled as one of the lampirs shook it vigorously. Then a frustrated growl came from inside the kitchen.

Emily gave the others all a quick thumbs-up sign from the roof of the outhouse and disappeared.

Ben went next. He was halfway up when one of the lampirs bellowed with rage and punched a hole through one of the solid oak panels of the kitchen door.

A clawed hand reached through and grazed Jack's shoulder. He leaped away with a yell.

Ben reached down for the blue hat-box and then passed it to Emily, out in the lane.

"Hurry," hissed Filip.

The kitchen door shook violently and the sound of splintering wood filled the night. The lampirs were breaking the door down.

Ben reached down again, this time for the Dhampir Tome in its oil-cloth wrapping. A dog began barking frantically in the next street, and Jack saw the kitchen door bulge on its hinges, as a strong shoulder slammed against it.

"You next, Jack," Filip urged.

"You'll be right behind me?" Jack checked.

"So close, you'll feel my breath on the back of your neck, my friend!" Filip assured him.

The kitchen door finally gave way with a loud crash.

Jack glanced back to see four or five lampirs stagger into the yard. They headed for Filip, their faces twisted with hunger and their fangs glistening.

Jack was about to jump back and help his friend when he noticed that Filip was fumbling with something: a tinder box. There was a cracking sound and orange sparks lit up the yard. A tiny flame flickered, and the lampirs cowered, terrified. But several more were coming through the door behind them. They all stood in the narrow doorway, unable to move backwards or forwards.

"So," Filip said calmly to the lampirs. "I think you are

up the creek and haf no paddle." And with that, he threw the tinder box at the nearest lampir. It struck the creature's dry and dusty grave-clothes. Jack saw the cloth smoulder for a moment, then burst into flames.

And then Filip was pushing Jack upwards, and they were both on the roof of the outhouse. Below them, lampirs staggered into each other as the fire leaped from one to the next. Bright flames flared, igniting dead skin, dry hair and lace collars. Soon each and every lampir was on fire, and the air was filled with the acrid stench of burning.

Further along the street someone opened a window and shouted, "*Pozar!*"

"Quickly," Filip urged. "They are shouting 'Fire!' We must go before they alert the city's firemen."

Jack went over the wall and landed like a cat, knees bent. Ben and Emily reached up to steady Filip as he came down beside them, slapping the dirt and snow from his hands. "Now then, my friends. Are you sure it is to the Hotel Syrena you wish to go?"

Emily nodded. "Absolutely certain," she said firmly.

"What if Edwin Sherwood does not believe our story about lampirs?" Filip wanted to know. "After all, he is a man of science, like my brother!"

"Uncle Edwin might be a man of science," Ben told him. "But after coming face-to-face with the vampire-god Camazotz last year, there's no doubt he'll believe in lampirs."

Filip nodded. "Then follow me," he said, picking up the blue hat-box. "I know a short-cut to the hotel."

Apart from a small lamp on the night-porter's desk, the hotel was in darkness when the small party of friends arrived some thirty minutes later. All four were weary, and slightly dishevelled, from their brisk walk through the narrow backstreets and dark alleyways of Warsaw.

Filip was shivering from the cold, having left his jacket stuck under the now-splintered kitchen door. Ben had offered to lend him his own, but Filip had his head. "I am a native of this country," he said proudly. "I am used to our wintry weather."

Even so, he looked very relieved when they finally walked into the warm, silent foyer of the Hotel Syrena.

Jack nudged Ben. "Should we wake old Sleeping Beauty there?" he asked, nodding at the night-porter. The man had his chin on his chest and was snoring softly, mouth open.

"I think we'll have to," Ben muttered. "This hotel has two hundred rooms. It could take us all night to find Uncle Edwin's!"

"No need," Filip said cheerfully. "Last time we were here, I overheard the clerk say the room number to the bell-boy." He began to make his way towards the stairs. "Our destination, my friends, is Room 105."

Still clutching the Dhampir Tome and the blue hat-box, the four hurried up the grand staircase and down a long corridor, their footfalls muffled by thick red carpet.

"Here we are," Ben said at last. "Room 105." He rapped on the door.

They waited in silence for what seemed like an eternity, until at last the door opened a crack. Uncle Edwin peered out. He was tying the cord of his dark-blue dressing gown and his greying hair was rumpled. He rubbed his eyes blearily. "Ben? Emily? Jack?" He frowned when he saw that Filip was there too. "I think you'd all better come in."

Edwin Sherwood's room was small but pleasantly furnished, with a bed, a leather couch, a writing desk and two armchairs. Long, tasselled, gold velvet curtains hung at the two windows.

Ben and Emily sat on the couch, the Dhampir Tome in its oil-cloth wrapping propped between them. Jack and Filip took an armchair each, Filip with the blue hat-box perched on his knees. Edwin Sherwood sat on the end of his bed and looked at them expectantly.

"Now, then," he said gently. "It's three o'clock in the morning. Do you mind telling me what all this is about?"

Ben heaved a sigh and glanced enquiringly at Emily and Jack.

"Go on," Jack said quietly. "You tell the story."

Edwin's eyebrows rose. "Yes, Ben. Let's hear it."

"Well, Uncle Edwin. Our trip to Warsaw wasn't just about sightseeing. We came because I was ill, and the only chance of a cure was here in Poland."

"That must have been quite an unusual illness, then," Edwin mused.

Ben nodded. "It was. I had something called 'lampir plague'. It's usually fatal within twenty-one days. But Filip's brother is a doctor, and he's been working on a serum."

"Lampir plague?" Edwin said, pursing his lips. "I suppose it's no coincidence that the word 'lampir' sounds very similar to 'vampire'?"

"No coincidence at all," Ben agreed grimly. He went on to tell Edwin all about their recent adventures, explaining about the severed hand, how they had met Filip Cinska, and how they had battled against, and destroyed, the lampirs in London.

Edwin Sherwood's gaze only left his godson's face twice. Once to look at the Dhampir Bell nestled in its blue hat-box, and the second time to watch as Filip unwrapped the Dhampir Tome from its oil-cloth.

At last, Ben fell silent.

"I wish you'd told me all this before," Edwin said gently.

"But we didn't want to worry you," Emily explained. "We never imagined that things would spiral out of control like this."

Edwin turned to look at Filip, his face grave. "So you think your brother Roman has managed to make a potion that turns ordinary people into lampirs?"

"Yes. I'm afraid so," Filip replied sadly. "And he has to

be stopped. But first I must figure out the incantation."
He patted the blue hat-box. "Using the Dhampir Bell and
the chant together is the only way we can stem the tide
of this lampir plague!"

Edwin stood up. "You're welcome to use my desk,
Filip," he said, moving aside papers, journals and
reference books. "I'm no cryptologist. As Ben and Emily
will tell you, I can barely manage to finish *The Times*
crossword, but obviously I'll help in any way I can."

"Thank you, Edwin," Filip said simply.

Edwin turned to Ben, Emily and Jack. Emily, Ben
noticed, was hiding a yawn behind her fist, and Jack
looked red around the eyes. They were all tired, and
Uncle Edwin's next words didn't surprise him one bit.

"Bed for you three!" Edwin Sherwood said firmly.
"You'll work better tomorrow if you get some rest
now. You take the bed, Emily. I'm going to work with
Filip. The boys will have to make do with the couch and
some blankets and cushions on the floor, I'm afraid."

Within ten minutes, makeshift beds had been
arranged. In his cosy nest on the couch, Ben fell asleep
far more quickly than he had expected.

CHAPTER TWENTY-ONE

Emily was awake at dawn the next morning. After only three hours of sleep, her eyes felt gritty, but she splashed cold water on them and ventured across to the writing desk. Filip and Uncle Edwin seemed to have made some progress on the Dhampir Tome.

"Your godfather is as much of a linguist as you are, Emily," Filip said, looking up at her with a tired smile. His face looked pale and bleak in the early-morning light, his eyes shadowed with grief for his brother. "Edwin's Latin is remarkable."

"Latin is an archaeologist's friend," Edwin Sherwood explained. "So many languages are derived from it."

Emily perched on the arm of Edwin's chair. He was slowly turning the pages of the Dhampir Tome. "May I see how you're doing?" she asked.

"Of course," Filip said, handing her a sheet of paper covered in fine scrawl. "Edwin and I have managed to translate the rest of the page you and I were working on – the page with the doodles, you remember?"

Emily nodded. "Yes, you thought you'd found some of the incantation. But there were parts you couldn't read because of the blood. Have you found the incantation somewhere else in the Tome?"

Filip shook his head soberly. "No, unfortunately not yet. But I *have* found some information about the ritual itself. You see here, where it mentions *The Speaking of the Rhyme*? This is an instruction of some kind, telling us how the incantation should be chanted. Take a look at it for me, Emily. Tell me what you think."

Emily leaned forwards to look at the Dhampir Tome. Meanwhile, Filip drew a fresh sheet of paper towards himself, dipped his pen into Edwin's ink-pot and began to write a letter.

Emily studied the page, aware that behind her Ben and Jack were waking up, yawning and stretching and muttering about breakfast.

"You can get breakfast on the way, my friends," Filip told them, as he pressed a piece of blotting paper on to the letter he'd just written.

"On the way where?" Jack asked curiously.

"Yes. Where are we going?" Ben added.

"You and Jack are going to take this to a place in Radska Street, down by the riverside," Filip said as he handed Ben the letter. "I have drawn you a map so that you can find your way easily. It is a foundry you want, and a man by the name of Mankus. I doubt he speaks English, so I have written all the instructions in Polish." He handed over some more papers. "This is a diagram of the new clapper I want Mankus to fashion for the Dhampir Bell," he explained, as Ben and Jack peered at the map and instructions.

Jack grinned as he studied Filip's diagram. "Right! The bell ain't going to ring if it don't have a clapper!" he remarked.

"That is correct," Filip agreed. "Forging such a piece may take all morning, but I hope that on your return Emily, Edwin and I will have pieced together the incantation." His face clouded and he hesitated for a moment. "Then we shall be ready to perform the ritual and stop my brother's lampir army," he added sadly. He turned away, obviously upset, and Emily thought she saw him dash a tear away from the corner of his eye.

Edwin Sherwood held out a brown leather wallet. "Ben, there should be enough money in here to pay Mankus and to get yourselves some breakfast on the way."

"Thanks, Uncle Edwin," Ben replied, tucking the wallet into his jacket pocket as Jack picked up the blue hat-box. Then they were gone, hurrying out of the door and along the hotel corridor.

Emily turned resolutely back to the Dhampir Tome.

Muffled in their coats and scarves, Jack and Ben hurried through the crowded streets of Warsaw. It took them more than an hour to find the foundry, which was in a small brick warehouse built almost underneath the River Wisla's only bridge. And it took another ten minutes of loud knocking to rouse the blacksmith, Mankus.

"*Czego chcesz?*" Mankus snarled, almost wrenching the door off its hinges and glaring out at them through bloodshot eyes. He was a giant of a man, with a thatch of coarse black hair that covered his head and most of his face, and ended in a bushy beard. He reeked of drink.

Ben thrust Filip's letter under the blacksmith's bulbous nose. "*Dziekuje* – thank you!" he said, with a hopeful smile.

Mankus grunted and snatched the letter, half-crushing it in one hand. He frowned, and squinted, and frowned again. Then he screwed the letter up into a ball, tossed it over his brawny shoulder on to the floor and slammed the door in their faces.

Jack and Ben stared at each other in dismay.

"Charmin'!" said Jack, rolling his eyes.

"What do we do now?" asked Ben.

"We make 'im change 'is mind," Jack replied flatly. He handed Ben the hat-box and pounded on the door. "Open up!"

But the door didn't budge. And soon, from inside, came a strange sound, like distant thunder.

"He's snoring!" Jack said, amazed. "Mankus has gone to sleep! We're stuffed now."

Ben nodded morosely. "I doubt we'll be able to find

another foundry in Warsaw. And even if we do, we'll never be able to make ourselves understood. Mankus has got Filip's letter explaining in Polish exactly how the clapper's got to be made!" He hitched the hat-box up and glanced back along the narrow, sloping lane that had led them down to the river and the foundry. "I suppose we'd better go back and tell Filip what's happened."

Unable to think of a better idea, Jack agreed and the two boys turned away. But they had only gone a short distance when the door to the foundry creaked open and a small voice said, "You, English – wait moment!"

Jack turned in surprise and stared at the cheerful-looking lad who now stood in Mankus's doorway. Jack guessed he was about a year older than himself and Ben, a small, skinny boy with dirty-yellow hair and a turned-up nose.

"I haf your letter!" the lad said, waving the piece of paper, which was now smoothed almost flat. "I am apprentice, name of Ivo. . ." he went on. Ivo's English was good, although strongly accented. "I do most of work here at foundry while Mankus drinks and sleeps. I can make clapper for you now – if you like?"

Jack felt a wave of relief wash over him. With a grin, he hurried back along the lane with Ben close on his heels.

Ivo led them through a stuffy little room, simply furnished with a table, stool, and rumpled bed, where Mankus lay sprawled on his back snoring loudly. At the back of the room was a stout oak door which led through to the foundry.

Jack and Ben found themselves in a huge room the size of a barn. The rough stone walls gleamed red in the light of a gigantic forge in the centre. An inverted brick funnel formed a chimney over the fire, and in one corner of the foundry an enormous heap of coal rose almost to the ceiling.

Ivo stuck Filip's letter and diagram on to a rusty nail sticking out of the wall. Then he donned a leather apron, spat on his hands, and selected the bellows from a variety of massive tools hanging on a rack beside the forge. Cheerfully, he applied the bellows to the smouldering fire until it glowed white-hot.

The dry heat filled the room. Jack could feel the sweat breaking out across his forehead, and a glance at Ben showed that his friend's face had turned as red as a tomato. It was too much after the raw chill of the Warsaw winter outside, and both shrugged off their coats and loosened their shirt-collars.

"What about Mankus?" Ben asked. "Won't he hear us?"

Grinning, Ivo shook his head. "Is no problem," he said cheerfully. "Always my master sleeps until midday, and then he staggers out to the tavern."

A short time later, Ivo put the bellows away and reached for an instrument that looked like a saucepan with a three-foot-long handle. "You are wanting clapper

165

for bell?" he asked. "I need... How you say...?" He spread his hands wide, and then brought them closer together again.

For a moment Jack and Ben stared at Ivo in confusion. Then Jack guessed what he wanted. "Oh! You need to measure the bell."

Ivo grinned and pointed to the workbench. Ben hurried to put the hat-box where the lad showed him, and Jack duly lifted the lid and took out the Dhampir Bell. It was a gleaming bronze dome about fifteen inches high. Firelight from the forge reflected off its smooth polished curves, giving it a warm glow. Around the rim was a line of carved letters, which Jack now knew to be Polish, interspersed with various religious-looking symbols.

Jack and Ben watched Ivo work, not quite sure whether the apprentice expected them to help. "Have you any idea what he's doing?" Jack asked Ben after a while.

Ben looked doubtful. "Well, I read about bronze casting once. It was a long time ago, I admit, but I remember that the founder has to heat the metal until it becomes a liquid. Then they pour it into a cast to get the shape, and cool it quickly by plunging it into a vat of cold water."

Jack nodded in the direction of a huge oak vat on the other side of the room. "Like that one?"

"I suppose so," Ben replied. "Then they have to polish

166

it and make it look as gleaming and beautiful as the bell."

Jack folded his arms and leaned back against the wall. "Casting, cooling, polishing. . . Reckon we're going to be here for some time, then," he said.

Ben nodded. "Couple of hours, I'd say."

In fact it was twice that, but by the afternoon the Dhampir Bell had a brand-new clapper, Ivo had a pocketful of money, and the boys had carefully wrapped the bell and clapper to stop it ringing, and trudged all the way back to the Hotel Syrena.

Emily met them at the door of Uncle Edwin's room. She offered them a plate of *pierogies*, little pockets of dough filled with melted cheese, and both boys eagerly helped themselves. Jack was suddenly aware that his stomach was grumbling loudly. He and Ben had completely forgotten to get any breakfast.

"Any progress?" Ben asked, putting the hat-box down on one of the armchairs.

Emily opened her mouth to reply, but over at the writing desk Filip flapped an irritated hand in the air.

"Ssh!" he hissed. "Silence!" He bent his head so close to the Dhampir Tome that Jack thought his nose must be touching the page. "I am trying to work this out. *Okrag*, that means a circle. . ." He muttered some more, and rubbed a hand through his hair.

"Poor Filip's exhausted," whispered Emily, looking worried. "I've tried to get him to eat something, or take a break. But he won't." She glanced at the empty cups littering the desk. "All he does is drink black coffee and rub his eyes. And we're still no closer to finding those missing symbols."

"Where's Uncle Edwin?" Ben whispered.

Emily looked even more worried. "A very official-looking gentleman came and asked him to go to an important meeting. He hasn't come back yet."

"*Okrag. . .*" Filip muttered to himself again. "*Chodzic w okregach*. Is this a riddle of some kind?"

Brushing *pierogie* crumbs off his fingers, Jack wandered across to the writing desk and glanced over Filip's shoulder. "The only riddle I know," he said, "is this one – Why is a dog like a tree?"

Ben rolled his eyes and flung himself down on the bed. "Because they both lose their bark when they're dead!" he said to the ceiling. "That's such an old one."

Jack grinned to himself. Then suddenly, as he continued to gaze down at the open page of the Dhampir Tome, he felt his heart begin to race. "Hold on – I've seen that before," he said, pointing over Filip's shoulder at the line of symbols which decorated the edge of the page. Smudges of brown obscured some of them, but others were clearly visible. "In fact," he said firmly, "I've been looking at it for most of the day!"

Jack could feel everyone staring at him in astonishment as he darted across the room and prised the lid off the hat-box. He lifted out the Dhampir Bell and held it up high, taking care not to let the new clapper hit the side.

"Look at the rim of the bell!" he exclaimed. "The symbols are just like the ones in the Tome!"

Filip stood up, almost toppling his chair in his excitement, and peered hard at the bell. "Goodness, my friend. I think you might be right!"

Carefully, Filip carried the bell across to the writing table. Together, he and Emily compared the symbols on the rim to the symbols in the Tome.

"It's true," Filip announced at last, in an awed voice. "The symbols are the same. The incantation is repeated on the bell!"

"Well done, Jack," Emily said, her eyes shining. "Now we can fill in all the gaps and work out exactly what the chant should be!"

A short time later the door opened and Edwin came into the room. He had a newspaper tucked underneath one arm, and he looked tired and worried. But his expression brightened when Ben told him that the rest of the incantation had been found.

"That's excellent news," he said, helping himself to a cup of coffee from the pot on a side table. "Can you perform the ritual now?" He looked round at them all hopefully.

But Filip shook his head. "I have partially translated it, but it has been written as some kind of riddle. Presumably to ensure secrecy!" He thrust his fingers

169

through his wild hair. "I keep coming across this word, *Okrag*. It means a 'circle', but it seems to bear no relation to the other words it is placed with. Honestly, I feel as if I myself am going round in circles!"

Edwin's hopeful look faded, and Jack suddenly knew there was something he wasn't telling them. "What is it, Edwin?" he asked.

Edwin glanced at Emily. "You remember the Secretary of the Royal Archaeology Society, who came to fetch me earlier? He had worrying news about a development in the city, and wanted to call an emergency meeting. There's a possibility that the symposium is going to be cut short."

Ben's eyes widened with surprise. "Why?" he asked.

Uncle Edwin took the newspaper from under his arm and unfolded it. "This is the afternoon edition of the Warsaw *Record*. I'm afraid lampir plague has made the headlines!"

Edwin handed the newspaper to Filip, who scanned the front page and translated: "The sickness has become an epidemic. The death toll continues to rise. People are being murdered as they try to flee the city, and all routes out of Warsaw seem to have been blocked. . . !"

Jack caught a glimpse of the horror in Filip's eyes as he glanced up at them.

"It says here that the editor of the *Record* believes that the authorities have ordered the road-blocks in order to prevent people from carrying the plague to other towns and villages. In effect, Warsaw has been quarantined."

"But it's not the authorities," Emily said quietly. "It's Roman Cinska and his lampirs. He plans to turn every man, woman and child in Warsaw into a soldier for his lampir army!"

Edwin took a deep breath. "And that's not all. This quarantine business is beginning to cause widespread panic. The chairman told me that there were riots during the night. In the west of the city a few buildings were set on fire, and shops were looted. And this morning, one of our own chefs here at the Syrena was driven mad with fear. He poisoned his wife and children, and then killed himself."

"That's terrible," whispered Emily.

Edwin nodded. "It's vital that the ritual is performed as soon as possible. It's the only way to stop the lampirs and cure the infected before anyone else has to die."

Filip put down the newspaper and hurried back to his desk. "If you are any good at solving riddles, Edwin," he said, "then Emily and I desperately need your help."

Jack shot Ben a keen look. "Reckon we're going to need a back-up plan," he muttered, "just in case this riddle can't be solved."

"That's exactly what I was thinking," Ben agreed. "Something along the lines of a big fire – like the one in the London docks last month!"

Jack nodded soberly. "And who better to ask for

171

advice on fires than a foundry apprentice? You and I had better go and talk to Ivo."

"But it will be dark soon," Emily said, looking worried. "The lampirs will be out, looking for blood."

"Then we'll take lamps and tinder boxes," Ben said firmly.

"And candles." Grim-faced, Jack picked up a small candlestick from Edwin's bedside table.

The boys were halfway out of the door when Filip suddenly thumped the surface of the writing desk with his fist.

"Going round in circles!" he exclaimed. "Of course. My friends, I have it!"

CHAPTER TWENTY-TWO

Filip explained quickly.

"In order to return the lampirs to their graves and imprison them there for ever, it is necessary to walk a circle around the area in which one wants the ritual to take effect. At the same time, one must ring the Dhampir Bell and chant the incantation." He clenched his fist excitedly. "Walk and chant. Walk and chant . . . in a circle all the way around the outside of the city!"

"Trapping the lampirs inside the circle!" Emily finished triumphantly.

"Sounds logical," Edwin said.

"What are we waiting for?" Ben cried. He couldn't understand why they were all still standing around talking. "We should go now. Before it gets dark!"

But Jack shook his head doubtfully. "Warsaw's huge," he pointed out. "Surely it would take all day to walk around the outside of the city."

Filip sighed. "You are right. It's now three o'clock in

the afternoon, and there is perhaps only an hour of daylight left," he said. He glanced at the window, where the wintry sun was sinking towards the horizon. "Polish winters mean short days in January."

"And we can't perform the ritual in the dark," Emily added. "We wouldn't be able to move for lampirs!"

Reluctantly, Ben nodded. "All right. So we start first thing tomorrow?"

Uncle Edwin looked thoughtful. "Wouldn't it make sense to use the last hour or so of daylight to make our way to a location on the very outskirts of the city? That way, we'll be in a position to begin the ritual at sunrise. The earlier we start, the more chance we have of finishing before dark."

"That's a very good idea, Edwin," Filip agreed. "But with the riots and the looting, I feel it needs to be a place of extreme safety. We cannot risk anything happening to the Dhampir Bell at this stage."

There was silence for a moment as they all considered this. Then Jack's face brightened. "The Monastery of St Wenceslaus!" he said. "It's built into the old city walls, and you can't get much closer to the outskirts of the city than that!"

"And it looks like a fortress," Emily put in excitedly. "High walls, strong gates, watchtowers and battlements! The Dhampir Bell will be safe there."

"Perfect." Filip began to wrap the Dhampir Tome in

its oil-cloth covering. "We will ask Father Zachariasz if we can stay the night there."

Edwin shrugged on his coat and strode to the door. "I'll go downstairs right away and organize transport."

It took the others only a few minutes to pack up the Bell and the Tome, and to put on their gloves, hats and scarves. Downstairs, Edwin had secured a Berlin carriage and soon the small party was on its way to the Monastery of St Wenceslaus.

Ben sat by the window with the hat-box containing the Dhampir Bell on his knees. He gazed out at the streets, surprised by the long queues outside bakeries and grocery shops.

"Everyone is preparing for a siege," Filip said quietly, following Ben's gaze. "They have all read the newspapers, and they are frightened. They want to make sure they have enough food to feed their families until this quarantine is over. They do not realize that hunger is not the only enemy they will face."

Ben shuddered. It was still daylight now, but as soon as darkness fell and moonlight struck the frozen earth, lampirs would rise from their graves and stalk the city seeking blood. "And while lampirs drink the blood of their relatives," he murmured, "Roman will be giving out his new serum and creating even more lampirs."

"Yes. . ." Filip looked thoughtful for a moment. Then he looked round at them all, his face grim. "I think we must go to the house and destroy my brother's

175

laboratory, so that he cannot create any more of his evil medicine."

Jack and Emily both nodded immediately. "Good idea," Ben said.

Ben saw Edwin glance out of the carriage window. The sun was sitting low in the sky, a dark red ball of fire above the snowy rooftops.

"It will be dark before long," Edwin said, with a worried glance at Filip. "If we go to the house, we could be taking the Dhampir Bell right into the heart of Roman's lampir operations."

Emily leaned forwards, her face set. "That's a risk we'll just have to take, Uncle Edwin."

The first thing Emily saw when the Berlin stopped outside the Cinska house was the abandoned landau. It was still at the side of the road, looking forlorn in the gathering gloom of late afternoon.

At once memories of the previous night's events came rushing back to Emily. Lampirs chasing the open carriage, the ill-fated landau driver, herself racing to wake the others and escape the house, even as lampirs slid in as shadows through the front door.

"Come on," Jack said briskly. He took her arm and helped her out of the carriage, almost as if he knew what she was thinking. "We've got work to do."

Edwin asked the Berlin driver to wait for them, while

Emily, Jack, Ben and Filip cautiously approached the front door.

"I will go first," Filip said in a determined voice, and he slipped his key into the lock.

The door swung wide, revealing the custard-yellow walls and the row of wooden chairs outside the consulting room. A faint tang of lemons and furniture polish hung in the air.

"Florentyna. . ." Filip murmured. "I hope she is all right."

Edwin joined them, and together they advanced into the hallway. As the front door swung closed, silence seemed to press in on them. A shadow flickered at the corner of Emily's vision and she felt her heart begin to race.

"Where do you think Roman is?" she whispered.

"Well, he's not in here," Jack said, peering into the consulting room.

Edwin cleared his throat. "Let's go straight to the laboratory. That's why we came, and we can't afford to hang around here any longer than we have to."

Filip nodded. "There is enough daylight coming in through the windows to make sure we are safe for now. Let us hurry." He strode down the hallway towards the basement steps, calling, "Roman? Are you here, brother?"

There was no reply, but Emily could have sworn she saw another shadow move out of the corner of her eye.

When she turned to look properly, there was nothing there. "Let's be quick," she said uneasily. "It'll be dark soon and we must get to the monastery."

Despite its whitewashed walls, the cellar seemed dark and cold. Emily could just make out the shape of the couch along one wall, and the workbench opposite.

"It's dark in here," Edwin muttered, glancing up at the single grimy window set high in the wall. "Did you say it was possible for a lampir to move around in a darkened room?"

"Only if there's no light at all," Emily told him. "A lampir can only take human-form indoors in daytime if the darkness is complete."

"Well then, we'd better make the most of the last few rays of sunlight," Jack said in a determined voice. As the others moved towards the workbench and began dismantling Roman's equipment, he dragged a chair across the room and stood on it to reach the window. As he cleaned away some of the grime with his cuff, a narrow shaft of daylight streamed in. "Better than nothing, I suppose," he muttered.

Systematically, they worked through the laboratory. Emily poured anything liquid down the sink, Ben emptied jars of powder into a coal scuttle, and Filip and Jack smashed glass beakers and phials. Edwin hurriedly disassembled the spirit lamp. As he did so, a little liquid seeped out and pooled on the floor.

Soon the laboratory looked as if a mad scientist had gone through it with a sledgehammer.

Emily was just pouring the last flasks of liquid down the sink, when a harsh voice boomed across the laboratory: "WHAT IN HEAVEN'S NAME ARE YOU DOING?"

Everyone froze.

Emily glanced back over her shoulder to see Roman standing in the doorway. He looked scruffy and unkempt, with stubble on his chin and a tea-stain down the front of his shirt. His spectacles were bent and cracked.

"What are you doing?" The doctor cried, staring around the wrecked laboratory in horror. "My life's work is ruined!"

Still holding a glass phial in one hand, Filip marched across to his brother. "Your life's work has been ruined by your own hand, Roman. We are simply trying to stop the damage you are inflicting on the people of Warsaw!"

Roman looked bewildered. "What are you talking about? I am a doctor. I heal people, not harm them."

Filip shook his head. "No, brother. Listen to me – by day you are Doktor Roman Cinska, but at night you become someone else."

*Some*thing *else*, Emily thought.

"Don't be ridiculous," Roman said flatly.

Ben took a step towards the doctor. "It's true," he said. "Remember the other day at breakfast, when my

179

sister said she'd seen you working down here during the night?" He shot Emily a keen look. "Tell him, Em."

Emily took a deep breath. "Roman, I *did* see you working here. So I decided to stay awake last night and see if you did it again. And sure enough, you came down to your laboratory and made a batch of serum. I followed you across the city and watched you give it to people who didn't seem to have the plague. Then you went to a cemetery. . ."

Quickly, Emily told Roman of the events in the graveyard, and how she had managed to escape from his army of lampirs. As she talked, Roman seemed to age before her eyes. By the time she came to the part about the way the new serum had turned healthy blood into lampir-blood, he was visibly shaken. His shoulders slumped and his face looked drawn and haggard.

"I made a bad medicine?" he whispered. "I turned my patients into *lampirs*? This cannot be true."

He began to pace back and forth in the gathering gloom of early evening, thrusting his fingers through his hair and muttering to himself.

"This is why you dream of lampirs, brother," Filip said gently. "The lampirs you see at night are no nightmare-creatures. They are a reality that your other half – your lampir-half – is creating and controlling."

"No!" Roman shook his head violently. "There are no such things as lampirs. I do not believe in this superstition!"

But even as he spoke, Emily could see that something strange was happening to Roman. As dusk advanced and blue shadows lengthened in the cellar, Roman seemed to grow less solid. For a split-second, he rippled into shadow-form. Emily recoiled in horror. But then the doctor was Roman again, a solid human, shaking his head and saying, "I am a man of science!"

Emily blinked. Were her eyes playing tricks on her?

But then Roman shifted into shadow once more, for longer this time. "I am building an army. . ." he spat, his voice suddenly inhuman and harsh. "You will not stop me!"

Then he was human again, wringing his hands and murmuring weakly, "No . . . please . . . no!"

"Dear God!" Edwin muttered, staring at the doctor in horrified fascination. "What's happening to him?"

"He seems to be battling with himself," Ben murmured. "I think his lampir-half is trying to gain control."

Filip darted forwards and seized hold of Roman's hands. "Fight it, brother! Fight this evil monster which inhabits your soul," he urged.

Roman blinked and peered at Filip. "F-Filip?" he whispered. "Where are you? I can't see you. My sight is hazy. There is a veil before my eyes. . ."

"The doctor's strength is fading," Emily said urgently. "We have to help him!"

"But how?" asked Jack.

Even as they spoke, the shadow-Roman came back. He seemed stronger this time. His black form shimmered and twisted, his shadow-hands slipped through Filip's fingers. "You cannot stop me," he snarled. "I shall overcome this miserable human body and then my might will know no bounds! I shall triumph – and I shall build an army fit for a *lord* to command!" Throwing back his head, the shadow-Roman let out a roar of mocking laughter. The hideous, mirthless sound seemed to fill the cellar, bouncing from the whitewashed walls until Emily wanted to scream and clutch her own ears to block it out.

At last the laughter stopped and the human Roman's voice hung in the air, disembodied, whispering, "So it's all true, then. Forgive me, brother. I did not believe you when you talked about lampirs, and it was my undoing. . ."

"Where are you?" Filip cried, looking around desperately. "I can't see you, Roman."

"He's not in human-form," Emily said fearfully. "His lampir-half is winning the battle!"

The laboratory was growing dark. Shadows flickered across the floor. Over by the workbench, Jack snatched up a tinder box, his face grim.

"Fight it, brother!" Filip bellowed, angry now. "Fight! You can be strong when you have to."

Something shifted in the corner of the room.

"I'm so sorry, brother." Roman's whisper was faint now. "Filip, you must stop the lampir army. . ."

There was a sudden pressure in the air that seemed to bear down upon them all from above. Then, abruptly, the shadow-Roman reared up before them, huge and inky-black, twice as tall as the real Roman had been. Horror-struck, Filip staggered backwards.

Emily caught a glimpse of an evil face in the gathering gloom – it was Roman all right, but an evil, demonic Roman with razor-sharp lampir fangs, and now it was taking physical shape. Raising his arms, the creature grinned at them. "At last I have defeated my weaker self. MY TIME HAS COME!" he boomed.

Jack struck a match against the tinder box. "Your time may have come, mate," he said calmly. "But you ain't exactly standing in the best place to enjoy it."

For a moment Emily was confused. But then she glanced down and saw that Roman was standing with one foot in the pool of liquid spilled from the spirit lamp. All Jack had to do was drop the lit match on to the floor, the liquid would ignite – and Roman would burn.

But before Jack could make a move against him, Roman flickered into shadow-form again – and vanished!

CHAPTER TWENTY-THREE

"Where did he go?" Ben cried, looking desperately around for a glimpse of the lampir-Roman.

"My brother is gone. . ." Filip murmured, sinking to the floor with grief.

"The doctor might have gone," Jack said, shaking his match out. "But look. . ." He indicated the shadows that still lurked in the darkest corners of the room. "His army is gathering."

"We have to get out of here," Emily said urgently. She seized the hat-box while Jack scooped up the Tome.

"Go!" Edwin cried. "I'll finish destroying the laboratory." He swept his arm along the workbench, sending everything that remained on it crashing to the floor.

Ben caught hold of the grief-stricken Filip and began to push him towards the door.

"But Uncle Edwin, we can't just leave you here!" Emily cried.

"You aren't leaving me," Edwin replied. He stamped on a rack of glass phials and shattered them. "I'm right behind you!" And he ushered them all firmly up the basement steps and out of the house.

The carriage came to a halt outside the Monastery of St Wenceslaus just as the first star appeared in the evening sky.

Ben stared up at the monastery, awed. Emily had been right when she said it looked like a fortress: towering red-stone walls, looming watchtowers and an enormous pair of oak doors kept out unwanted visitors. *If a building like this isn't lampir-proof, then nothing is!* Ben thought.

The subdued little group huddled together on the pavement as Edwin paid off the driver. Emily was clutching the Dhampir Tome and Filip had the blue hat-box. It gave Ben an odd feeling to see the carriage lumber away down the deserted street towards the city – because now they were alone.

"I hope young Brother Lubek remembers us," Filip muttered. He propped the hat-box on one hip and hammered on the huge oak door.

The small metal grille snapped open and a voice said, *"Tak?"*

An elderly monk peered out at them, his brown eyes wary within their pouches of wrinkled skin. He shook his bald head as he muttered something in reply to Filip's question, then the grille snapped shut again.

Ben frowned and turned to Emily. "I take it that's not 'young' Brother Lubek?" he asked.

Emily shook her head, anxiously glancing up at the deepening blue of the evening sky.

"What's going on, Filip?" Edwin enquired.

"He tells us to go away and find shelter elsewhere," Filip replied. "He is afraid to open the door – in case we are not what we seem."

"Not what we seem?" Jack stared at Filip incredulously. "He thinks we're lampirs, doesn't he? The fool. He only has to look at us to see we're human!" He reached past Filip and banged on the door himself. "Hey! Open up, mate – we ain't lampirs!"

Filip put a hand on Jack's arm. "No, my friend. The monk does not think we are lampirs."

"What then?" Jack said.

"He thinks we are looters," Filip said gently. "Thieves!"

"Well, tell him we ain't!" Jack started to pace up and down on the pavement, his face red with indignation. "Make him fetch Father Zachariasz – he'll remember us!"

As the night darkened around them, Filip rapped on the door again and shouted in Polish. A muffled voice replied, saying something that to Ben's ears sounded like *"Nie!"* which he knew meant *"No"*.

Then, above the arguing and the knocking, he heard another noise – a familiar sound which made his blood go cold. It was a low, rasping, guttural growl: the death rattle of a lampir.

"Jack, look out!" yelled Emily.

Jack's indignant pacing had taken him about six feet away from the group. He was just making his way back to them when Emily's cry alerted him to danger.

Wheeling round, he saw a tall figure approaching at a run. A white face loomed out of the darkness, fangs gleamed and claw-like hands reached for Jack's face.

Edwin, who had never seen a lampir before, stared incredulously. "Good *Lord*. . ." he breathed.

"No!" Jack shouted. He threw his hands up in front of his face to stop the lampir scratching at his eyes with its sharp, black fingernails.

But, suddenly, the lampir stopped. It backed away, groaning and snarling.

"What's the matter with it?" Ben gasped. He stared at Jack, his eyes wide with horror. "There's only one reason for a lampir to back off like that. *Have you been infected, Jack?*"

Jack's stomach clenched and he tried to remember if – or *when* – he might have been scratched. . .

But Emily shook her head quickly. "It's Molly's ring, remember?" she reminded Jack. "There's a legend in the Dhampir Tome which says that a person is immune from lampir attack, if they are wearing a piece of jewellery from a person who died of lampir plague," she told the others.

"Everyone had better stay behind me," Jack said, holding his hand up in front of him, fingers spread wide so that the lampir could clearly see the ring.

The creature was cowering. But two more ragged figures came loping out of the gathering shadows. One of them was a woman, with long golden hair and glittering emeralds hanging from her ears. She had obviously been a wealthy lady once. Now she snarled and bared vicious fangs.

"Filip, if there's anything you can say or do to get that door open, you'd better do it *now*!" Edwin muttered.

The lampirs closed in on either side, cutting off any chance of escape.

Filip renewed his frantic hammering on the door, shouting in Polish. Jack could just make out the words, *"Father Zachariasz!"* . . . *"Lampir!"* . . . and *"Pomocy!"* which he knew meant *Help!*

The lampir-woman was so close that Jack could smell the grave she'd climbed from. Mould and earth clung to the sleeves of her gown. She growled at him, but Jack held his hand steady and kept the ring where she could see it, and she didn't attack. Instead, she edged sideways, her milky gaze flicking from Emily to Ben and back to Jack.

Suddenly she lunged for Ben. He let out a yell and

dodged away. Jack reached out with his ring-hand, aware that he was leaving Emily and Edwin exposed.

Immediately the other lampirs saw the gap in their defences. One of them lurched forwards. He was an old man with a bald head like an egg. His striped shirt and high-waisted breeches looked almost new, and Jack guessed he hadn't been dead long.

As Jack turned back to face this latest threat, the old man seized his chance and attacked Emily. But Edwin was there, delivering a powerful punch to the old man's jaw which sent him flying.

"*Father Zachariasz!*" yelled Filip desperately, pounding on the monastery door.

Just then, a terrible roaring and howling met their ears, and all at once twenty or more lampirs appeared from the right, streaming along the deserted street towards the friends. Some wore rags. But others looked as if they hadn't even been buried yet, and Jack knew they must be some of the newest members of Roman Cinska's lampir army.

"Fire," gasped Ben. "We need fire!"

More lampirs appeared from the left, some of them loping like wolves, bent almost double as they dragged their hideous, rotting flesh towards the monastery.

"We need more than fire, mate. We need a flamin' miracle!" Jack exclaimed.

There was nowhere to run. The friends were surrounded. Filip was still hammering his fist on the door, but he turned to face the onslaught as the others flattened themselves against the oak panels on either side of him. The stench of death in the air was so strong that Jack's stomach lurched.

"Pomocy!" the friends screamed. *Help!*

The nearest lampir reached out as if to pluck the blue hat-box from Filip's arms. . .

But, at that moment, Filip fell away backwards into the building, as one of the massive oak doors to the Monastery of St Wenceslaus was wrenched open.

CHAPTER TWENTY-FOUR

The friends tumbled through the door, into the Monastery of St Wenceslaus.

"My dear friends, I am sorry for the delay in offering sanctuary," said Father Zachariasz, breathlessly, as he slammed the door behind them.

He had made a torch by wrapping an oil-soaked cloth around the end of a length of wood, and he held this high as he peered at them, his face anxious. "I gave orders to barricade the doors and admit no one. But when I heard your voice, my son," he gently touched Filip's arm, "I came immediately."

A young monk in a brown cloak – Emily saw the ginger hair and realized it was Brother Lubek – began to shoot enormous bolts across the doors, locking out the lampirs. Outside, she could hear their howls of frustration.

"What about the shadows?" Ben asked, scanning the edges of the door. "They could come underneath – or through the gaps!"

But Brother Lubek shook his head. He kicked a row of sandbags against the foot of the door, and then quickly dipped a paintbrush in a huge copper bucket, standing over a fire. It was full of a cloudy liquid.

"Melted candle wax!" Emily exclaimed, as the young monk brushed it thickly all around the door. The cold made it turn solid immediately, sealing the gaps.

"We have had to learn new methods of defence," Father Zachariasz said darkly. "This is an enemy like no other."

"You can say that again," Jack muttered.

"Follow me." Holding the flaming torch high to light their way, Father Zachariasz hurried across the courtyard ahead of them. "The Monastery of St Wenceslaus is a large and complex series of buildings. Although our windows and doors can be sealed against shadows, nothing can stop a lampir from climbing the walls. Last night, they came seeking blood and several Brothers were taken." He shuddered. "Tonight, rather than try to defend a large area, we plan to seal ourselves inside one small building – and pray that, by morning, it has not become our tomb!"

The little party ducked beneath a stone archway as the abbot led them into the shadowy cloister garden, full of overgrown herb bushes and dead grass. In the middle was a small stone chapel. Dozens of monks were gathered at the door, their faces pale with worry above their brown cloaks. Some of them held flaming torches, and the firelight flickered across the garden.

One hurried forwards and spoke in a trembling voice to Father Zachariasz. It was the elderly monk who had refused to let them in. He darted a fearful glance at the newcomers, but Father Zachariasz patted the old man's shoulder and spoke comfortingly to him.

"Brother Cezar is afraid that you are lampirs," Brother Lubek explained in his halting English. "Our abbot is telling him you hold the key to our salvation. Is this true?"

Emily, still clutching the Dhampir Tome, nodded quietly as they all entered the little chapel. "Filip has translated the incantation which will imprison all the lampirs in their graves," she explained. "We're going to start the ritual at dawn tomorrow."

Relief washed over Brother Lubek's face. "So this could be the last night that we come under attack? Tomorrow, all will be well?"

"Fingers crossed," Jack said cheerfully. Then he looked around at the inside of the chapel and gave a low whistle. "Ain't this something else!"

A thousand candles flickered like fairylights, lighting up the colourful frescoes which had been painted on the walls. Hundreds of serene-faced angels gazed down from the ceiling, their huge creamy-white wings spread wide. Gold-leaf murals and carved ivory shrines gleamed in the alcoves where monks quietly knelt to pray. Just inside the door, an oil lamp burned brightly on a shelf.

"It's beautiful," breathed Emily, awed by the feeling of calm and tranquillity inside the chapel.

She followed Filip and Edwin as they made their way to a pew at the front, near the candlelit altar. As she placed the Dhampir Tome down next to Filip, Emily noticed that a few of the sick people from the hospital wing were stretched out on makeshift beds in a nearby alcove. They were all asleep, their faces pale in the candlelight.

"Wait!" Ben's voice echoed down the chapel, edged with panic. "Look!"

He was pointing out through the open door. In the distance, several dark hunched figures were loping across the cloister garden towards the chapel. Others were scrambling over the monastery's red-stone walls. Some of them were armed with knives and clubs. All of them were lampirs!

"Barricade the doors!" cried Father Zachariasz.

"No, wait! I've got a better idea," Ben cried. With steel in his eyes, Ben seized the oil lamp from the shelf by the door. "It's going to be a long night. I think we should send as many lampirs to their doom as possible! Come on, Jack!" He ran outside and began setting fire to the grass and bushes around the chapel.

Emily saw Jack nod grimly. He plucked the torch from Father Zachariasz's hand and rushed to help Ben.

"Be careful!" Emily cried. Her heart in her mouth, she

watched from the doorway as the boys put Ben's plan into action.

The lampirs roared with rage, flailing their arms as Ben doused every herb bush, clump of grass and skeletal shrub with lamp oil. Jack followed in his wake, thrusting his torch into the shrubbery and jumping away as the bushes burst into flames.

Soon every twig and leaf was burning brightly, the conflagration fanned by the light breeze. Showers of sparks rose into the night sky. Some landed on the lampirs like tiny fireflies. The ragged clothing smouldered for a moment, and then burst into flames. Several lampirs burned, disintegrating into piles of ash. Panicking, the others shifted into shadow-form and scudded away.

Quickly, Ben and Jack completed their circle of the cloister garden and met at the chapel door. But before they could get inside, a lampir loomed out of the shadows and hurled itself towards them. Emily yelled as it seized the sleeve of her brother's coat and tried to drag him backwards across the courtyard.

"Have this instead, mate!" Jack cried, and reached over Ben to thrust his torch straight into the lampir's face. The desiccated flesh went up like a firework, popping loudly as the flames took hold.

Ben ducked away from the burning lampir and both boys dashed headlong into the chapel. Slamming the doors, Brother Lubek began to seal the cracks with his pot of melted candle wax.

The friends hurried to peer out of the chapel windows at the burning lampirs, and the monks knelt to pray.

Then there was silence.

Several hours later, Emily woke with a start. She blinked, rubbed her eyes and wondered how long she had been asleep.

"Em, sorry to wake you, but it's our turn for the watch," Ben said softly.

Then Emily remembered – they had decided last night that it would serve no useful purpose for everyone to stay awake. Edwin and Father Zachariasz had organized hour-long watches, taking the first slot themselves. The watch patrolled the chapel, checking the wax seals and ensuring that rows of candles and flaming torches were kept burning at every window, to frighten away any lampir that came close.

Now Emily could see that Uncle Edwin and the abbot had wrapped themselves in woollen cloaks and were lying on two of the wooden pews.

With Ben beside her, Emily crept past the sleeping figures and made her way over to Filip. He was sitting by one of the chapel windows in a pool of candlelight, scribbling something on a scrap of paper.

Filip looked up as Emily and Ben approached. "I have made everybody a copy of the incantation," he said.

"You will need them for the ritual tomorrow. I have been thinking that we shall need to take turns, just as with the night-watch. It will be a long and tiring job to walk all the way around the city, especially ringing such a heavy bell."

"Good idea," Emily said, taking the scrap of paper he held out. "Is there anything else we need to know?"

Filip nodded. "Whichever one of us completes the ritual must ring the bell three times to close the circle. The lampir legions will only be imprisoned in their graves when the third and final chime of the Dhampir Bell dies."

Emily nodded to show she'd understood. Then she and Ben went to take over the watch from Jack and Brother Lubek.

"All is quiet," whispered the young monk, and Jack gave her a quick thumbs-up.

But no sooner had they turned away, than a crashing sound echoed through the chapel. A rock flew through the air, hit the floor, and came to rest beside Emily's left foot. She stared in horror – one of the stained-glass windows had been smashed, and a lampir's hand was reaching through the jagged hole.

Grabbing the nearest torch, Emily ran to the window and touched the flame to the lampir's sleeve. It caught fire instantly, flaring yellow and orange. With a howl, the lampir dropped away.

Immediately, another took its place.

Ben was there this time, igniting the creature's hair with a deft touch. Behind him, Jack stood poised for the next onslaught.

Brother Lubek dashed away down the aisle towards the alcove where the sick people lay. He came back with some shredded fabric. "Bandages we brought from the hospital wing," he gasped. "We can lay them on the windowsill and set fire to them, create a barrier of flame!"

"That's a great idea, Lubek!" Ben said. "But we're going to need more – lots more!"

Emily helped him lay the bandages along the windowsill. They touched a torch to each end and stood back as the flames licked inwards. But within moments the bandages had burned away to soft white ash, and another lampir face appeared at the hole in the window.

Emily gritted her teeth and jabbed her torch at it.

"Cloth burns too quickly," Father Zachariasz called from the other side of the chapel. "Someone help me smash up a pew. We need to make more torches."

Edwin and Filip were already on their feet. They began tearing the legs from the pews and wrapping the ends of them in cloth. Brother Cezar hurried forwards with a pot of lamp oil, and Filip dipped his torch into it.

The torch flared into life the moment Edwin touched a candle-flame to the oil-soaked cloth.

"Here, take it," Filip said, passing the torch to Jack. He immediately began to make another, and another, and another. Soon, the air inside the chapel was thick with smoke, and the acrid stench of burning oil.

Everyone took turns to defend the window with their makeshift torches. Wielding flames was hot work, and by the time Emily was able to leave the window and sit down, she could feel sweat trickling down her back. Beside her, Ben's face was smudged with soot.

Then came the sound Emily had been dreading. A second window exploded inwards – this time on the far side of the chapel – and the rock that came flying through was the size of a beer keg. A lampir began to clamber through the gaping hole. The lampir was a young woman who had obviously once been pretty, but now her ringlets hung in lank strands around her face, and the tip of her nose had rotted away. Her fangs glittered in the torchlight.

Emily leaped to her feet, Uncle Edwin beside her. He was yelling and wielding his torch like a cricket bat. His long legs covered the ground fast and he reached the young woman just before Emily did. He jabbed his torch at her ragged pink dress.

The lampir-woman staggered as flames engulfed her, but she was swiftly replaced by other lampirs. A constant stream of walking dead scrambled through the hole in the stained-glass window, oblivious of the comrades that had fallen before them. Emily and Edwin took turns with their torches, managing to set light to all but one of the lampirs.

The lampir they missed ran helter-skelter across the aisle, tipping pews with its flailing arms. It had once been a man with smoothly-oiled hair and a neat moustache. Growling and snarling, the lampir-man hesitated near the makeshift beds where the sick were sleeping. But then Emily saw him veer away. She guessed instantly that he had recognized the sick as plague-infected. Now the man was heading for a group of monks who cowered by the altar.

Emily saw Filip grab up a three-branch candelabra. He dived between the monks and the lampir, landing on his stomach and skidding along the smooth stone floor. Just as the lampir-man reached for the nearest monk, Filip touched the flames to the lampir's black-striped trousers.

The creature burned fiercely, twisting in agony before collapsing into a heap of grey grit.

Emily turned back to the window. A lampir had managed to grip the jagged glass around the edge of the hole and pull hard, widening the gap with a sickening cracking sound. And then, several feet to Emily's left, a third window exploded inwards.

Before anyone could react, another snarling lampir heaved itself in through the blue and green shards of stained glass. This creature had been dead so long that Emily could only guess whether it had once been a man or a woman. In one skeletal hand, the lampir carried a long wrought-iron spike that looked as if it had once been a fence post.

Old Brother Cezar let out a cry of rage. "That was the stained-glass window depicting Our Sacred Lady!" he roared. "It was three hundred years old. You demons have no respect!" And with that, he launched himself at the nearest lampir.

Suddenly he stopped in his tracks.

And then Emily saw why. The lampir had thrust the fence post out in front of him, and Brother Cezar had run on to the wrought-iron spike, impaling himself.

A dark stain bloomed on the front of his robes, and blood trickled from the corner of his mouth. As more lampirs crowded in through the hole in the Sacred Lady window, Ben ran to help Brother Cezar. But it was too late for the elderly monk. He was dead.

Emily turned back to the window she was guarding. She was aware of Jack still battling at another window on the other side of the chapel, and of Edwin rushing to help her keep the lampirs at bay.

And then Father Zachariasz turned a haggard face towards them. "The lamp oil has run out," he cried. "There is no more fuel."

"We're doomed!" one of the younger monks sobbed, and threw himself down on to his knees to pray.

But Emily had no time to panic, for another lampir had appeared in front of her, snapping its fangs so close to her face that she felt its gruesome breath on her cheek. Trembling, she thrust her dying torch between its ribs, and felt a jolt of satisfaction as the creature went up in flames.

But there were more behind it, a never-ending stream of lampirs that she couldn't hope to hold back. The chapel was filled with the stench of burning flesh. Black smoke caught in Emily's throat. All she could hear was the young monk's prayers – and Jack shouting.

At first, what Jack was saying didn't register. Then, to her surprise, Emily saw the lampirs slipping into shadow-form and sliding away from the chapel, across the burnt-out remains of the cloister garden.

And all at once, Jack's words made their way into Emily's head: "I can see the sunrise!"

The terrible night was over.

CHAPTER TWENTY-FIVE

"*From the Earth you came. And so shall you return. Sleep the Eternal Sleep. And trouble the living no more,*" chanted Ben, and he rang the Dhampir Bell for what felt like the millionth time. He was actually chanting in Polish, but Filip had told him the English meaning of his words.

The deep, fluid chime of the Dhampir Bell spoke for itself, the vibrations of the chime seemed to roll outwards like a wave.

As he chanted the ritual, Ben thought his arms had never ached so much in his life before. The bell seemed to be getting heavier by the minute, as if all the power and force of the ritual was weighing down the bronze dome. And according to Filip, they were still only halfway round the city.

They had started by the chill light of dawn, filing out across the burnt grass of the cloister garden, each clutching the slip of paper Filip had given them. At the monastery gates, a solemn Father Zachariasz had bid them farewell. He had sent Brother Lubek with them. The young monk was clutching an armful of wooden torches just in case twilight came early.

Emily had begun the ritual, chanting the Polish words of the incantation clearly as she rang the bell and walked slightly ahead, with Ben and the others fanned out protectively behind her. Slowly, the weak winter sun had risen in the sky, streaking the clouds with pink.

The little group had walked quickly along the cobbled streets and unpaved roads. At first everywhere was deserted, the shops closed and the houses shuttered. But soon the city had begun to wake. Clerks began to make their way to their offices, muffled in scarves and hats against the cold. Housewives and serving-girls scurried to the shops. And a few citizens came out of their houses to stare at the small group: three children, two men, a monk and a *bell*?

A party of students had jeered at them, shaking their fists and shouting. Filip had quickly said that the students thought they were superstitious fools.

But there were also people who seemed to wish them well. An old woman in a woollen shawl had run after the little group, kissing the crucifix that hung around her neck.

"She is blessing us," Filip had explained. "She says that she hopes our efforts work . . . and that she is sure that the old ways are the best."

Soon it had been Jack's turn with the bell, then Filip's, Edwin's and finally Ben's. And yet still they were only halfway round the city.

Ben trudged forwards. Slowly the afternoon wore on. Ahead, the watery sun began to slip towards the horizon.

"What time is it?" Ben heard Emily ask, eventually. She was squinting at the sky. "It seems to be getting darker."

Jack shook his head. "I heard a chapel bell tolling three o'clock not long ago. We should still have an hour of daylight left."

"Thick cloud gathers over the east of city," Filip said quietly. "A storm is following in our footsteps – see?"

It was true. Behind them and to the east, the sky was dark and bruised-looking, filled with rolling clouds that sat so low over the city they seemed to brush the rooftops. The air was charged and heavy, as if full of a thunderstorm that wouldn't break. The cloudbank seemed to be thickest just behind them, as if the storm was gathering within the area where the chant had been said.

And clouds weren't the only thing that followed them. Ben glanced back over his shoulder and saw that a long line of people walked in their wake: men, women, children, the young and the old.

Ben felt like the Pied Piper.

"Here, mate," Jack said, reaching out. "Let me take over."

Ben realized Jack must have noticed how tired he was feeling. Gratefully, he relinquished the Dhampir Bell and let Jack stride ahead, while he fell into step beside Emily and Brother Lubek.

His sister was watching the gathering shadows with a grim look on her face. "I think this is more than a storm," she said at last. "These shadows that are lurking in doorways and on street corners – some of them seem human-shaped. But there are no humans near them!"

"Do you think they're lampirs?" Ben asked.

"I do," Emily replied. "They're attracted by the Dhampir Bell, just as they were in London."

Ben nodded, remembering. Lampirs found the chime of the bell irresistible. They were drawn to it, mesmerized by its melodious ring. In London, the friends had used this to lure the lampirs to their death in the dockside fire.

This time, however, Ben realized it could be their undoing. If the friends didn't complete the ritual before the sun went down, the lampirs would shift into human-form and devour them all. Shuddering, Ben glanced at the sky. "We're safe while it's daylight," he said firmly.

"And I have these torches," Brother Lubek put in. "Perhaps I should light them? We could form a protective shield of fire so that the ritual can be completed."

But Emily still looked sombre. "There's something heavy in the air," she said. "Something evil. I can feel it!

The lampirs know what we're doing – and they hate us for it."

"They can't hate us as much as we hate them," Ben replied flatly.

Just then he felt a small, gloved hand slip into his. Startled, he turned to see a girl of his own age with dark hair and eyes. He recognized her immediately. It was Grazyna, one of Roman's patients who had come to the consulting room a few days ago with her sick mother.

Grazyna smiled shyly at Ben and he smiled back. Glancing over his shoulder at the line of people following them, he saw more familiar faces: little Albin, Florentyna, even Ivo the apprentice. But all around them were dark shadows, as more and more lampirs converged on the group, attracted by the deep resonance of the Dhampir Bell.

"I think perhaps we should light those torches," Filip said to Brother Lubek. "It won't hurt to chase these shadows away."

Edwin dug in his pocket for his tinder box. Then, quickly, they all gathered around Brother Lubek and lit the first torch, then used it to light the next, and then the next. Ben passed the torches back along the line. As the bright flames flared, he noticed that the lampir-shadows cowered fearfully, and relief flooded through him.

They pressed on, through narrow streets and along the banks of the River Wisla. With the torches burning brightly, the lampir-shadows kept their distance. But still more of them seemed to be answering the call of the bell. Their numbers swelled until the ground was thick with thousands of ominous black shapes.

"Roman and his legions were busy last night," Filip muttered grimly, looking at the shadows.

Eventually, Jack passed the Dhampir Bell back to Emily. She walked forwards determinedly, now on the last stretch of the circle.

The sun was sinking lower in the sky, and Ben began to fear that they wouldn't be able to close the circle before the sun set. But then, at last, he looked up and saw something which made his heart lift. At the far end of the shadowy street was a cluster of brooding towers and parapets: the Monastery of St Wenceslaus! Its red-stone ramparts looked as dark as blood against the late-afternoon sky.

Ben squeezed Grazyna's hand. "We're nearly there!"

Beside him, Jack grinned jubilantly. "There's Father Zachariasz in the doorway," he pointed out.

"He's holding a burning torch to guide us," added Filip.

Abruptly the stormy grey clouds rolled forwards over their heads, shutting out the last of the daylight. On the far horizon, the watery orange sun dipped low in the winter sky. Its cold light touched the rooftops, and Ben felt a sudden, sick dread. It was sunset.

Lampir-shadows moved restlessly, rippling across the

fronts of buildings and slipping along the icy cobbles. They could sense their time was near.

And then the sun turned blood-red and sank below the rooftops. Darkness fell. There was no dusk, no twilight. It was just as if the lights had gone out, Emily thought. She focused on continuing the ritual, and rang the Dhampir Bell. Its melodious chime rang out, mesmerizing in its resonance.

And in that instant, the black shadows around her shifted into human-form.

CHAPTER TWENTY-SIX

"Look out!" Jack and Ben rushed forwards, and Emily found herself surrounded by people waving flaming torches. But beyond the protective ring of fire, she could see hundreds – no, *thousands!* – of hideous lampirs. And every one of them was armed.

Some had once been men, hulking and muscular with strong hands that now clutched knives and staves. Others had been peasant women, their hair wrapped in colourful strips of fabric, their powerful arms now raised to brandish hammers, axes and pitchforks. Emily saw one lampir-lady in long white evening gloves and gown, with a tiara still fixed in her elaborately-curled hair, and a small girl in a long white dress and a little lace bonnet. Dusky purple streaks marred their pale, newly-dead flesh. Lamplight gleamed yellow on their vicious fangs.

She kept going, forcing herself to say the words of the chant without faltering. If she let the lampirs distract her, then she knew the whole of Warsaw was doomed.

The lampirs pressed closer, their milky-white eyeballs rolling as they gazed hungrily at the Dhampir Bell.

Emily rang the bell again, and shouted the next line of the chant, struggling to hear her own words above the lampirs' howls.

Someone screamed. Emily glanced over her shoulder to see that it was one of their followers. He had fallen and was immediately seized by a lampir who sank sharp fangs into his arm and sucked hard, drinking his blood. But Edwin stepped in, stabbing the creature with his torch and setting it alight. Fire leaped from its clothes to its hair, and the lampir burned, screaming. Jack hurried to help the victim, keeping lampirs at bay by wielding the gold ring on his middle finger. They shrank back, and Emily was silently thankful for the power of Molly's ring.

She moved onwards, calling out the chant and ringing the bell. And then, above the clamour, she heard a strident voice which turned her blood to ice.

Filip recognized the voice, too. "It is my brother, Roman!" he cried in horror. "He is saying 'Kill them all and bring me the bell!'"

The moment they heard their leader's command, the lampirs attacked, surging forwards in a great wave. Steel clashed against wood as axes and knives hit the wooden torches.

But Jack, Ben, Filip and Edwin stood firm, with young Brother Lubek beside them. They wielded fire – the deadliest weapon a lampir could face – and the torches were still burning brightly. When one lampir caught fire, the flames leaped quickly to the next. Dozens were vanquished.

And Emily pushed on towards the monastery. She could see the portly figure of Father Zachariasz holding his torch aloft as he urged the friends on.

Emily gasped out the words of the chant and rang the Dhampir Bell again. All around her, she could hear the rasping death rattle of the lampirs. She saw Jack and Ben battling furiously, stabbing their torches left and right as lampirs tried to duck beneath the fire and slash at their ankles with sticks and pitchforks. Above the din, she could hear Roman Cinska's evil voice shouting commands in Polish, but she couldn't see him.

Emily dragged her thoughts away from Roman. She knew she had to concentrate on reaching the monastery and closing the circle. It wasn't far now. She was almost there. She could see Father Zachariasz's kindly eyes, and hear his encouraging words. Any moment now she would be able to ring the Dhampir Bell three times – just as Filip had instructed – and the lampirs would be driven back to their graves, for ever!

Then, suddenly, without warning, a huge shadow slipped beneath Emily's feet and raced ahead of her. It reared up in front of her, blocking her sight of the monastery, and then solidified into human-form.

It was Roman Cinska – but not Roman as Emily had known him in life. This Roman was huge, perhaps seven feet tall with broad shoulders and powerful arms. His face was deathly-white, like a corpse's, but his eyes were bright with unholy life. Emily felt as if those dark blue eyes were burning into her.

"Admit defeat, Miss Cole," Roman hissed. "I *will* have the bell!"

Defiantly, Emily stared back at Roman, still chanting as loudly as she could.

He roared with fury and raised his arm high above his head. For one moment, Emily thought that he had simply swiped the air with his clawed hand, but then she caught a glimpse of steel, flashing in the torchlight as it flew through the air.

Roman had hurled a knife. And it was heading straight for Emily's heart.

Time seemed to slow as Emily stared at the knife. And then Filip launched himself into the air, throwing himself in front of Emily, and time sped up again. The knife hit Filip squarely in the chest with a dull thud. Emily cried out in horror as Filip fell to the ground, his hand clutched around the hilt of the blade.

Roman Cinska threw back his head and laughed.

"Filip, no!" Ben cried. He and Jack fell to their knees beside their friend. Around them, the lampirs closed in.

"Get back, you demons," shouted Brother Lubek, sweeping his flaming torch through the air. Edwin stood back-to-back with the young monk, valiantly trying to keep the protective ring of fire intact.

Filip lay at Emily's feet, blinking in surprise as his life ebbed away. "Stay strong, my friends. . . Close the circle. . ." he whispered

"Come on!" called Father Zachariasz. "Hurry to me!"

"Filip," Emily mouthed, distraught.

"Emily, please. *Finish . . . the . . . ritual. . .*" Filip gasped. And then his head lolled back and his lifeless hand slipped away from the hilt of his brother's knife.

He was dead.

Fury gripped Emily and she felt strength and resolve flood through her. Lifting the Dhampir Bell, she rang it again and continued the chant in a high, clear voice. Then she staggered forwards, stepping over the body of her friend to close the circle.

Standing at the monastery doors with Father Zachariasz, Emily rang the Dhampir Bell three times, just as Filip had told her. And as she did so, she felt its power tingling through her hands and coursing up her arms. The bell's bronze curves seemed to glow with an inner light.

Ben and Jack joined her and the friends waited breathlessly for the last echoing chime to fade. As it did, the clouds overhead seemed to boil in the sky. Thunder rolled and boomed around the city. A great gust of icy wind picked up over Warsaw, a howling gale that shrieked between buildings and ripped the slates from the rooftops. It came screaming towards the friends, an arctic blast that stung their eyes and tore at their hair like frozen claws.

"Stand firm!" shouted Father Zachariasz.

The lampirs cowered. Then the great wind began to suck the creatures backwards, away from the monastery and across the city. The lampirs switched to shadow-form, writhing and twisting as they merged into one stormy sea of shadows, trying to resist the power of that mighty wind. But it was impossible. Shrieking and howling, they were whipped across the ground towards their graves, while clouds of grey ash – the remains of the vanquished lampirs – swirled up from the cobbles in the bitter wind.

Emily searched frantically for Roman, but he was lost in the storm of shadows.

And then, without warning, the wind dropped. A great stillness settled over the city. All the lampirs had vanished, and there was utter silence.

Emily was suddenly aware that the power had gone from the Dhampir Bell. It was just an ordinary church bell again, a dull bronze dome. But the ritual had worked. Warsaw had been saved.

Emily clutched the bell tightly to her chest, staring at Ben and Jack. Jack's face was smudged with soot from his torch, and Ben's jacket was torn.

"Blimey," muttered Jack.

"It's over," Ben murmured, shaking his head in disbelief. "You did it, Em. You closed the circle."

Edwin smiled and gently took the bell from Emily.

And then Emily looked down at Filip, and felt her heart twist with grief. Their friend was gone. Brother Lubek was covering the body with his own brown cloak and murmuring a short prayer.

Father Zachariasz placed a gentle hand on Emily's shoulder. "Filip Cinska was a brave man," he said softly. "He will be buried with honour, within the grounds of the monastery. And every evening at dusk, the Brothers of St Wenceslaus will light candles and say prayers. We shall give thanks for the sacrifice Filip has made."

"Thank you," whispered Emily. She felt something soft and cold brush her cheek, and dashed it away with the back of her hand.

Jack frowned. "I smell snow. . ." he said.

Ben rolled his eyes towards the heavens. "Jack – how many times –" But he broke off as something soft and cold touched his face. White flakes were falling softly from the sky, settling on everyone's hair and shoulders.

It was snowing!

EPILOGUE

"Congratulations, Mr Sherwood," said the Chairman of the Royal Archaeology Society, shaking Edwin's hand vigorously. "That was a triumphant closing speech!"

"Thank you, sir." Edwin smiled, flushed with pleasure.

Ben grinned at Emily and Jack, who grinned back. Despite the terrible events of the past few days, the symposium had ended on a high note, and rapturous applause had greeted Edwin's speech. The delegates had filed out of the lecture hall, and were now circulating in the foyer of the Warsaw Assembly Rooms, champagne glasses in their hands.

"So this is champagne," Jack said, wrinkling his nose as he peered into his tall, fluted champagne glass. "It's all fizz and not much else!"

Emily raised her glass. "A toast," she suggested. "To Filip, our friend."

"To Filip," said Ben and Jack together.

* * *

A short time later, the three friends were standing with Edwin on the wide, stone steps of the Assembly Rooms. They had muffled themselves against the crisp night air in scarves, gloves and coats. A row of horsedrawn carriages idled at the kerb, waiting to take the delegates to their hotels and boarding-houses.

"Hotel Syrena?" the doorman said to Edwin. "Very good, sir!" and he gestured to the nearest cab.

A thick blanket of crisp white snow covered everything in sight, making all the spires and domes of Warsaw look as if they were part of some giant iced cake. Ice crystals glittered in the flickering light of a dozen glowing streetlamps. On a nearby corner a merry crowd clustered around a man selling hot roast chestnuts, and somewhere a girl's voice was raised in laughter.

"The city's bustling tonight," Ben observed.

Uncle Edwin nodded. "The Grand Theatre has opened its doors for the first time in weeks, and so has the Opera House."

Emily was watching a family pushing a wooden barrow piled high with household goods. "It looks as if all the people who fled the city are returning, too," she said with a smile.

"Funny how the snow makes everything feel festive," Jack mused. "It's like Christmas all over again, ain't it?" Ben didn't respond and Jack nudged his friend's arm. "Ben. . . ?"

But Ben wasn't listening. His attention was caught by a party of drunken revellers who had lurched into view on the other side of the busy street. They were laughing and calling to each other in Polish. One of them was taller than all the rest, his broad shoulders swathed in a long black cloak. He stayed at the back of the group, half-hidden. But Ben felt his heart begin to pound. He would know that face anywhere. It was Doktor Roman Cinska.

"Em! Jack!" Ben cried urgently, pointing. "Look over there. It's Roman. . ."

But even as the three of them gazed at the group of revellers, the tall man in black seemed to shimmer and disappear into the crowd.

"Are you sure it was him?" Emily asked.

"I thought it was," Ben replied slowly, staring at the spot where the figure had been. "We had better just hope that I was wrong."

"Well, it has been known," Emily said with a laugh. "Now, cheer up!"

Ben banished the figure from his thoughts and turned round just in time to see Emily throw a snowball at him. It struck him on the nose, which made Jack laugh and Emily clap her hands in delight.

"Hey!" Ben cried and was just about to throw a snowball back at his sister, when Edwin called. "Come on!" he said. "Our carriage awaits."

The carriage summoned for them by the doorman had

drawn up at the foot of the steps. It was a beautiful, open-topped landau, painted brilliant red, with a shiny black roof that was folded back. Harnessed to the front was a proud-looking chestnut horse wearing leather blinkers. Strings of silver bells jingled from its bridle and scarlet ribbons fluttered in its mane.

The friends all looked at each other in amazement, and Emily laughed with delight.

"We're going home in style," Jack said with a grin.

"We certainly are!" Ben agreed.

Brushing the snow from his hands, Ben helped Emily up into the carriage beside Jack and Uncle Edwin. Then, to the tinkling sound of bells and laughter, the friends were whisked away across the fairytale city of Warsaw.

Look out for...

Vampire Plagues 1: London
Vampire Plagues 2: Paris
Vampire Plagues 3: Mexico
Vampire Plagues 4: Outbreak

VAMPIRE
plagues

Emily put aside *David Copperfield* and stared at her brother, wide-eyed with surprise. "Ben, what on earth's the matter?" she asked. "You look as if you've seen a ghost or something."

"Or *something*," Ben said with an edge of panic in his voice. "Look!" He held out his hands, palms downwards and fingers outstretched. Every nail was tinged with a dusky shade of blue, as if each one was bruised. At first glance the discolouration did indeed look like ink, but Jack knew immediately that it wasn't. This was something much, much worse.

"Blue nails are the first symptom of lampir plague," Jack whispered hoarsely.

Ben nodded. "I've been infected!"